COUREURS DE BOIS

COUREURS DE BOIS

A Novel

BRUCE MACDONALD

Cormorant Books

This is a first edition.

Canada Council for the Arts | Conseil des Arts du Canada

The publisher gratefully acknowledges the support of the Canada Council for the Arts and the Ontario Arts Council for its publishing program. We acknowledge the financial support of the Government of Canada through the Book Publishing Industry Development Program (BPIDP) for our publishing activities.

Printed and bound in Canada

LIBRARY AND ARCHIVES CANADA CATALOGUING IN PUBLICATION

MacDonald, Bruce, 1966 July 12–
Coureurs de bois / Bruce MacDonald.

ISBN 9781-896951-72-0

I. Title.

PS8625.D625C68 2007 C813'.6 C2006-901864-2

Cover design: Angel Guerra/Archetype
Text design: Tannice Goddard, Soul Oasis Networking
Cover image: Michael Wilson/Getty Images
Author Photo: Igor Shpigelman
Editor: Marc Côté
Printer: Webcom

CORMORANT BOOKS INC.
215 SPADINA AVENUE, STUDIO 230, TORONTO, ON CANADA M5T 2C7
WWW.CORMORANTBOOKS.COM

For a kind purple orchid

The first person who, having fenced a plot of ground,
took it into his head to say this is mine
and found people simple enough to believe him,
was the true founder of civil society.

— JEAN-JACQUES ROUSSEAU

Money-lust has always existed, but not in the history
of the world was it ever a craze, a madness,
until your time and mine. This lust has rotted these nations;
it has made them hard, sordid, ungentle, dishonest, oppressive.

— MARK TWAIN, MARCH 14, 1905, *MARK TWAIN'S LETTERS*

PART ONE

SPRING

DREAM

IN COBB'S DREAM THE sky was black and there was no hope that light would come through. It was not night and it was not day. It was some place between the two.

He was in the exercise yard by himself. There were no other inmates and no guards on the ground or in the towers. He did not know how long he had been in the yard and he did not know how long it would be before somebody came for him. On the ground lay a pair of wire cutters. His first thought was that it might be a trick. He knew the white man could be tricky. If he even picked up the wire cutters he could be charged with attempting to escape. He turned from the cutters and walked away to the far end of the exercise yard. He walked all the way around the square enclosure. He was back beside the wire cutters. He looked both ways and behind him, then quickly bent down and picked up the wire cutters and put them into the back of his pants. He walked the yard, along the fence again, and again he saw nobody.

One side of the enclosure bordered the highway and the other three bordered the woods. He went to the side, where the fence was closest to the woods. He looked around again and still saw no one. He removed the wire cutters and quickly began to cut the mesh fence. His hands tightened and loosened again and again, each cut bringing him closer to freedom. He began to perspire. When the last of the links was cut he pushed through the mesh and stepped outside the prison. He hardly believed it. Where is everybody? he wondered. Then, as if in answer to his question, the red lights in the towers went on and an alarm sounded. Oh shit, he thought, there's no turning back now. There was nothing in the Criminal Code called "half-assed prison break," only prison break. He had to run. There was no way to avoid the charge. The deed was done. The fence was cut. He was not thinking. He was dreaming.

He should have remembered that there were degrees in sentencing. If he had dropped the cutters, stayed inside the yard, placed his hands behind his head and dropped to his knees, the guards might have looked the other way, but he was not thinking clearly, and he was not aware of his reality as dream and dream only, and so he ran.

He ran like a caribou on the ice fields, chased by a pack of wolves, but he would not give himself up to this pack. He was not a sacrifice to the Creator. It was a sacrifice to the bureaucracy of the white man and his queen. His heart pounded in his chest. His breath lapsed on him. He broke out in a heavy sweat. The cold of the place, the cold of the woods, was more pronounced on his moist skin. For a while he heard nothing. Then he heard the dogs. They were going to hunt him like an animal. His only chance was to get to water, to jump into swift water, dissolve his scent, and float down current with his head just peeking out for air, but there was no water to be found. He could not see any, hear any, or smell any. He started to panic when he heard the dogs close behind him. The guards were on horses. The guards were keeping pace with the dogs. If the dogs caught him, the guards would catch him. He begged for water. He ran down an embankment. He found none. He began to despair. Despair had not visited him for some time.

There was a dog right on him, nipping at his heels, and then he saw a horse turn around in a grove in front of him, a rider atop it.

He stopped dead and then felt a hard object hit him in the back of the head. He dropped to his knees, clasped his head. He was bleeding. He looked up and there were four riders around him. They looked down at him, and he stayed on his knees. He kept his hands behind his head — the position — and waited for the handcuffs to be snapped onto his wrists. When they didn't come, he looked up to see one of the guards stringing a noose over a thick tree branch. A terrible fear choked him but he remembered that they couldn't hang him. It is against the queen's law. Two guards forced him onto his feet and one put the noose around his neck. A rider pulled him up into the air. His hands weren't tied, so he was able to get his fingers into the rope. But there was no way he was going to be able to pull the rope from his neck. The rope was tied to a tree. He heard a whistle and the dogs disappeared with the riders back up the embankment. They were going to leave him there to die slowly. He urinated in his pants. He could barely pull any breath into his lungs and he realized it was only a matter of time. Being a fighter, he would grapple with the rope until he was dead. A horrible death.

He heard the sound of a hideous bird, a crow, and he felt a vibration in the rope. There was a crow pecking at the rope. If he could hold out long enough the Creator might spare him. He dug his fingers in so tight that the skin ripped and tore, but, as the Creator wanted it, he was saved. The crow did its job, and he fell to the ground. He looked up to where the crow was perched on a branch.

Cobb woke suddenly. The dream was clear. He was no longer the idle spirit wanderer. He had been adopted by Crow. A mission had been given to him. The dream was a contract. How could he see it as anything else? All contracts come from dreams because all ideas are dreamed in the places between the seasons, behind the wind, on the dark side of the moon. It was a contract. He was wet between the legs. He had wet himself in the dream. Crow wanted to make sure he remembered the contract when he woke.

VISION

WILLIAM TOBE WAS TOLD he had an ulcer. He was twenty years old and he had an ulcer. The doctor said that it was a peptic ulcer and that it could be cured with antibiotics. Will was given a prescription, but he did not fill it. He had heard a lot of bad information about antibiotics. He had listened to a five-part series on CBC Radio One about bacteria and antibiotics. Experts speculated that a new antibiotic-resistant bacteria would sweep the planet. The point of the series, as Will digested it, was be wary of antibiotics because they have been overused.

Will was a precocious young man. He had skipped two grades and entered university at sixteen and would have a degree before the end of this twenty-first year. When he was first told about the ulcer, he thought for sure that he had placed an inordinate amount of stress on himself. He had pushed himself too hard. His body was just doing its job. Then the doctor told him that such notions were now seen as medical myths, and that a peptic ulcer was caused by a bacterial infection. This caused Will long hours of research on bacteria. There were good and bad bacteria in the body all the time. Bacteria was needed, and he thought this was fascinating.

While researching, he found material on Stanley Burroughs' master cleanse, and he decided that he would do it for eleven days. The instructions were to drink water with lemon, maple syrup and cayenne pepper for eleven days straight, as much as he wanted. The purpose was to shut down the internal food processing factory and clean out the pipes. It said on the Internet that someone on the fast would continue to defecate right up until the eleventh day. A laxative herbal tea was required every evening, and that was the only deviation allowed from the lemon drink. The Internet site said that some practitioners had sustained the fast for one hundred days, and some monks for the full forty days of Lent every year. There was also a mention that it might help with ulcers. Will decided to do the fast.

After going to the store for a few things, Will returned to his dormitory on the campus of the University of Ottawa. He had been there for nearly four years and lived alone. He was getting a degree in economics. His sister was a financial analyst and his father was an economist-lobbyist with a right-wing think tank in Ottawa. William was following in the Tobe family business, and money was a business with a great future. Where can it go? His father had asked him when he was sixteen and deciding what to study at university — where can money go? It was indeed a good question, and Will had recognized it as such when it was asked. He had insisted on living on campus, and not in the family home, which was within a thirty minute walk of the prime minister's residence. He returned home on Sunday evenings for dinner, where his laundry was still done for him.

There had been headaches the first day of the fast, and he almost quit, but the second day got better, and the third even better, and by the fourth day of the fast it was like he was floating on a cloud. He had tremendous energy, was sleeping only five hours a night, and there were more and more vivid and remembered dreams; it was like he was waking up in sleep every night after the fourth day of the fast. On the seventh night his mind was electric. Everything was so clear, so perfectly clear. It all made sense. He turned on the bedside lamp and squinted. Even with the light on, the dream world was grabbing him with all its force. There was tremendous well being and love. He grabbed a notebook off the dormitory night table and wrote it all down.

1. a stream
2. a bright light
3. a crow
4. a crucifix
5. a black bear
6. a stone
7. purple flowers.

He turned off the table lamp and put his head on his pillow. He had his last exam that morning. He was happy about this, and he knew the ulcer was gone. He knew what he was going to do when school was finished.

TWELVE THOUSAND

COBB HATED THE DOWNTOWN. He hated the little busybodies with a sense of mission. He hated the suits, the skirts, the haircuts, the hair colours, the ties, the sidewalk conversations. He walked into one of the large, shiny buildings, one of the big cocks they put into their world, a large erection to remind them they weren't supposed to think about fucking everything that moved, weren't supposed to think about jamming their throbbing hard cocks into every moist wet place that moaned and begged. Cobb hadn't forgotten to fuck everything that moved. It was a part of his mission. There was sperm in his body. That sperm was part of his overall consciousness, part of his overall person. In fact, Cobb had thought about almost nothing else since he'd been released from prison. He went up the elevator to the twenty-second floor, into the office of Alexander Campbell, QC, which he knew to mean Queen's Counsel. What a bullshit expression, he thought for the half second it took him to open, almost unhinge, the large wood door. What the fuck had the queen done for him? What the hell did he care for some German bloodline living in the lap of luxury on the island of the Britons? They were no better than the French, the Jesuits, the Dutch, or any of the other bastards who had wandered the world in wooden boats, pushed by the wind — how could the Creator have given them wind — and pushed into the lives of others.

Catherine Campbell worked the reception. It was a family operation. She almost jumped out of her seat when she saw Cobb. Most people did. Cobb looked like he meant business. He was business.

"Randall Seymour," he said.

"You have an appointment?"

"No, I just thought I'd drop in and say hello."

"Are you being sarcastic?"

"No."

"You really just dropped in to say hello?"

"Yep."

"Are you here to see Alexander or Craig?"

"Who is Craig?"

"He's my brother. He passed the bar last year and he's working for my father now."

"I didn't know the queen had so many Scots in her counsel."

"Excuse me?"

"Did you fart?"

"I beg your pardon?"

"Why did you excuse yourself?"

"I'll get my father."

"That might be a good idea."

She used the speaker phone, so as not to appear secretive or rude, Cobb suspected.

"Yes," came the deep voice from the other end.

"There's a Randall Seymour here to see you."

"Send him in."

She pointed down the hall and said, "Second door on your left."

Cobb turned and strode down the hall and went into the second door on the left. Alexander was behind his desk. He smiled and stood when Cobb entered.

"How are you, Randall?"

"Not too bad."

"Just out?"

"A while now, a short while."

Alexander gestured for him to take a seat. He did and dropped into a large leather armchair, of which there were two in front of Alexander's large oak desk.

"Why didn't you come and see me right away?"

"I don't know."

"So what can I do for you?"

"I want to be a Freemason."

"A Freemason?"

"A Freemason like you."

"How can I help with that?"

"Let me hang out with you. Take me to all the secret places. Teach me the secret handshakes, and get me a seat on the Toronto Stock Exchange."

"What?"

"They say the Campbells murdered the MacDonalds in their sleep, and that's why your name is shit in Scotland."

"Randall, is this a joke?"

"I don't know. Do you feel like laughing?"

"Not really."

"I guess it's serious, then. If it wasn't, we both might feel pretty fucking uncomfortable right now."

Alexander hung the words in his mind for a second then burst out laughing.

"You're insane, Randall."

"I don't know what's funnier, that comment in and of itself, or the fact that you're giving free advice."

"Who is your parole officer?"

"I don't know. Some guy named Paddy in Parkdale."

"You haven't checked in yet?"

"Nope."

"You could land back in prison for that."

"It costs them a lot of money to keep me in there."

"It's all about the money then?"

"Isn't it?"

"And justice."

"Justice? What the fuck is that?"

"Right and wrong."

"Some tribes built longhouses and planted maize. Some raided the ones that planted maize because they hadn't made their own contract with the earth. You're just working for the tribe that raids, except you don't do it shooting arrows from underneath a galloping horse. You do it with math, accountants, actuaries, the illusion of authority."

"What the hell are you talking about?"

"Nothing, I guess. Anyhow, I came by to say hello, see how you're doing and say, 'No hard feelings.'"

"No hard feelings?"

"You know, the over billing?"

"Over billing?"

"I did the math in jail and I figure you took me for about twelve grand."

"Randall, if that's why you came here I think I'm going to have to ask you to leave."

"Okay. I'll come by your house on Saturday and we can finish our conversation then."

"My house?"

"Yes. Forest Hill Road, Forest Hill. I can come by the house."

"You know where I live?"

"Don't you?"

"Randall, I have to caution you, this sounds like a threat."

"What part?"

"All of it."

"Wanting to talk to my lawyer who charged me forty-eight grand for a two-week trial is threatening?"

"I meant your tone."

"This is the same tone I always speak with."

"What do you want?"

"I already told you, twelve grand."

"You can't have it."

"It's just a question of you giving it or me taking it. It's your decision, Alexander."

"I don't have that kind of cash handy. My car is insured, and my bank card won't give more than a thousand dollars in a single transaction. How would you take it?"

"All right, you got me. There's no way I can get twelve grand off you. So what I figured is I will skip the money system and take what the twelve grand meant to me and exact that price on you."

"And what is twelve grand worth to you?"

"I'll go to your house in the dead of night, when your fat ass is in bed, and I'll take your dog, then I'll kill your dog, then I'll eat your dog, or I'll stuff him and mail him back to you."

"I'm going to call the police now, Randall."

"Okay."

Randall sat there as still as stone and stared into the hazel eyes of his lawyer. Alexander picked up the phone. He dialled nine, one, one and waited for the operator to announce her presence on the other end of the line. His breathing was laboured and he started to sweat at the brow. He glanced up from the phone and Randall was still staring right into his eyes, no blinking, no readable emotion. Alexander Campbell, QC, was a man who had learned how to read people. Blank people frightened him. He hung up the phone.

"Fuck, Randall, this is insane. I'm your lawyer."

"Twelve grand."

"When?"

"Three days, this bank account."

Randall pushed a piece of paper across Alexander's desk. It had a transit number and a bank account on it.

"Put it all in here. If it's not there in three days you'll never see me again and you'll never know how or when or who or what, or any of the other questions that make charges stick."

"Okay."

Randall stood and left the office. Alexander inhaled suddenly and deeply. Apparently, for several moments during the latter part of Randall's visit, Alexander had forgotten how to breathe. His brow was hot and moist, and he felt a bead of sweat run down his temple. Alexander Campbell, QC, had one dominant, unspoken thought in his consciousness: That dog-eater scares the shit out of me.

Going down, the elevator was quick, and Cobb hit the street with the powerful and purposeful stride of a mountain cat. Alexander Campbell, QC, was his first finished chore as a free man. Cobb got into a beat-up old Ford 150 and started the drive back to the Gladstone Hotel. There was a cover on the pickup and it was loaded with cigarettes. It was a little over week since Cobb was let out of Warkworth Institution. There had been no car to pick him up. He had left Warkworth with only one half-full duffel bag that he had carried over his shoulder.

The day he had been released he had walked under an ash- and smoke-coloured sky, knowing that it could rain, but not worrying. His boots were good. His denim jacket was a little less than the weather called for, but he could get his mind off that. The time in prison had done him well. He was well-fed and larger than he was when he went in. He had put on nearly twenty pounds and taken three inches off his waist. Prison was better than Jenny Craig for Cobb. His crime didn't warrant Warkworth. He should have been at some camp somewhere, weaving baskets under a tree, and buttering homemade muffins brought by Mennonite volunteers, but they wanted to teach him a lesson. They wanted him to remember his experience. His arrest sheet was too full for their liking. Cobb was a drain on their finances, and, if they truly were a compassionate society, Cobb must have become such a sad sight for them that they just had to put him away for a while, not look at him anymore, either that or risk breaking their hearts. It was a great gamble, this compassionate society.

Conspiracy to defraud the Canadian government was the charge. Alexander Campbell, QC, had not prepared Cobb's defense. Cobb probably could have defended himself better. The queen fought dirty. It was like fighting a bear without a hatchet. A cheap, dirty, loaded fight, as far as Cobb was concerned. Her strategy was purely economic. The queen knew the value of an embargo. With absolute control there was no need to go to war. The queen went after assets, froze bank accounts, and put liens on property. All the resources required to fight the queen were taken away before the fight even began. It cost three hundred dollars an hour for Alexander Campbell, QC. Cobb had learned that the hard way. Law wasn't like any other trade in the white man's world. They kept law invisible. It was like a spirit world they consulted. They put on robes and spoke in a ritualized language. They gestured with meaning, seeming to summon unseen spirits into the brightly lit rooms with high ceilings. Alexander Campbell, QC, made a treaty with the queen. Cobb had to do two years and a day because he had no more money for Alexander Campbell, QC. Cobb learned there is little difference between money and justice in the Dominion of Canada.

The judge handed down the sentence. Indians went to prison like the queen's people went to university. It was a rite of passage. A lot of Indians had to look at shadows on dark walls for years of their lives, exploring the cave of the white man's bureaucracy by the light of their spirits only. Cobb had cousins in prisons all over Ontario and Quebec, from both his mother's Ojibwa band north of Peterborough and his father's Mohawk band near Cornwall.

Cobb used his time well. He studied the white man's sacred books and learned how they looked into the invisible world of law for the spirit of judgment. It was from this Great Spirit that they took much of their counsel as a people.

The charge had many sides and many forms. There were boxes and boxes of notes from RCMP officers, a lot of surveillance, and many statements from informants, with whom Cobb had bartered tobacco, a commodity the queen said she controlled. The earlier you make treaty with the queen the better the terms, Cobb had learned. The queen showed mercy for cooperation.

Income tax evasion was a sham. Income tax itself was a sham. The government had only mandated it during the war, brought to bolster the coffers and support the war, a white man's war in the white man's tribal motherland, Europe. It had nothing to do with Indians, and the Income Tax Act had nothing to do with Cobb. It came a few years after the Bank Act, and not many people made the connection. It was subtle. Taxes were the result of banking, the government banking, the interest on their debt. That was the key — their debt. There were a lot of people in prison who could see this clearly, which made Cobb wonder if prison wasn't some kind of deeper education, a place where the truth could be told because there were no more illusions. Fluorescent light all the time equals the end of illusions. It becomes harder and harder to lie to yourself when you're living under fluorescent lights.

Bartering was an old language for the First Peoples. In jail, Cobb realized that economics was in his blood. Trade surpluses and trade deficits, productivity indexes, gross domestic product, currency valuation — it was all just barter. The white man's spirit of judgment had many words. This spirit of judgment consumed words, and it was never sated. It was a demanding spirit. It had no limit on its growth. The more it ate, the bigger it got. The further it spread.

It was true that Cobb had sold cigarettes tax-free, but tobacco had always been the commodity of the North American Indian. The white man stole it from the Indian and made billions of dollars on luxury taxes and other excess taxation they said was to curb the health-care spending in a socialized medical system, spending caused by smoking-related ailments, but it was a sham. It was the bankers, Cobb had learned, who had sent him to prison. The money the Canadian government said he defrauded was really money belonging to the banks. The government was just collecting for them. It was a system of control. The whole modern world was a system of enslavement.

The Creator had put mischief in the world because people were supposed to learn from mischief. Fear was the language of the Creator for people who had forgotten how to live. The money was worthless, a token of barter, a measure of alleged wealth, a confidence game. The white man had commodified it as well. Its true value could not be measured, and because money was the measure of all other things, except the compassion they alleged in their society, the white man could not accurately measure the grains or hides needed for the seasons. It was sometimes too little or it was sometimes too much. Excess food in one village rotted while another village starved. They called them upturns or downturns, bulls and bears, but to Cobb it was just smoke and mirrors, a guess at best, a sham. The white man's whole life was a sham, and it revealed to Cobb the depths of the white man's corruption. The white man would sell his own sons and daughters into servitude.

Cobb knew that the white man was no longer a thing that could be seen. The white man had liberated himself from the pigmentation of his skin, from his sex, his hair, his age, and his place. The white man was an idea, like money, a commodity, the most prosperous human exchange. People from all over the world came to Canada to live like the white man. The white man could appear in a thirty-year-old Guatemalan bank teller. She didn't even know she was a white man. Most people who are possessed never know they're possessed. That is the power of spirits, and Cobb knew this before he went to prison.

The white man's system was not to be reviled. It was to be understood. Cobb had realized that only in understanding it completely could it be beaten, and so he had set his mind to the complete understanding of the white man's system, and he soon saw that the chink in the armour was fear. The white man could not really live in the world, as the world demanded people live in the world, in subservience to the Great Spirit, accepting the coming and going of prosperity, security, life itself. The white man had made contract against the Great Spirit. Contempt was the white man's prayer. If I must die, then fuck you, the white man said to the Great Spirit. Lazarus was the hope of their fear, as was Jesus Christ.

But there Cobb was, alive and well, and living in an apologetic culture that allowed Indians reserves, welfare, medical and dental care, processed food, and the right to hunt within the guidelines set out by the Ministry of Natural Resources. Cobb wanted to run in their woods, learn their ways, let the spirit of the white man into him, but only a little, as a kind of inoculation, a little bit of the disease to develop an immunity against it. He was afraid that he did not have the right to do what he wanted to do. The Mohawk and Ojibwa way was harmony with environment. If he attacked their environment, would that be a surrender to the spirit of the white man? Would it be the surrender of his free and true spirit? This he did not know, and it caused him hesitation. Cobb hated hesitation. All things move in a circle. All things come around to a level playing field sooner or later. The oppressed becomes the oppressor. The slave becomes the master, and then it all goes around again.

When he got out, Cobb had tried hitchhiking on the highway, but he knew it was unlikely that he would be picked up. At a solid 245 pounds, and with jailhouse tattoos on his neck, a long scar down his right cheek, his raven hair braided and resting like a long horse tail on his back, he looked every bit the Mohawk warrior that was his father's heritage. The road went on for over a kilometre before it bent and disappeared. It had snaked like that for the two hours he had walked it. He had kept his eyes on the gravel and maintained his steady shuffle through the grey day, occasionally looking into the thick wooded area beside the highway. It had occurred to him that he was just south of the 401, the highway that would take him to Peterborough and his mother's land and people, the Ojibwa reserve, a pristine model of modern Indian living with cable television, microwaves, pickup trucks and designer jeans.

The band was well managed, and that was largely due to Cobb's grandfather, a converted Catholic who, at eighty-eight, had the mental acuity of a government auditor when it came to numbers, balancing books and allocating revenue for band expenses. The band policed themselves, and when the Ontario Provincial Police did come on their land it was only after getting the permission of Cobb's grandfather, who would meet the cruiser and escort the constables to the house they were looking for and the Ojibwa to be questioned. His grandfather would then act as de facto counsel for the Ojibwa, offering his advice on which questions the Ojibwa should answer and which he should decline. Cobb's grandfather had a grade-six education, but had been a lifelong learner. His grandfather never missed a visit with Cobb, every two weeks, despite the long drive to the prison.

Cobb had looked up at the sky, then down at his watch. He had turned off the side of the road and into the woods. The ground had been wet in parts. The green had been coming in, but winter was not yet forgotten. Every kind of tree he had grown up with was there. He had missed trees. Prison had a spiritual side if it had caused him to miss trees. He would never miss trees again. Cobb had marvelled at the innocence still in him at twenty-eight. There were moments when all of the sounds were heard as one sound, and it was to Cobb the voice of the Creator. He had missed the message of the trees — turn toward the light. He had stopped in the woods and observed the moment, recognizing it as sacred. Only the Creator could show him his true self. And the Creator had spoken to him then and there, in the beautiful birdsongs, the day peeking in on the dark forest floor through the loose network of branches, buds and leaves, and the marvellous sound all around him. All his thoughts and worries had slipped away. He'd started to walk through the brush again, not as a man, but as a tree, turned to the light, so completely itself that it required no reflection.

He'd had no food, no sleeping bag. He had walked. That night he'd slept in the middle of the woods, somewhere between Highway 401 and the Ojibwa reserve, and the next day he'd awakened with the sun and began to walk again. He had made a stop at his birth ground, said hello to his people, made some business arrangements, then driven his Ford to Toronto, set himself up with a room. After a few days, he'd gone to see Alexander Campbell, QC.

Cobb made his first sale, a carton of cigarettes, to the front desk clerk at the Gladstone Hotel. His whole room was taken up with boxes and boxes of cigarettes. He had to find a storage place. He filled up a black hockey bag with cartons of cigarettes and left the hotel to begin the door-to-door canvassing that would start his business from scratch. Before he left, he burned sweet grass. The room he was staying in was the same room where his mother had died twelve years past, when he was sixteen.

FROGS

DOROTHY, THE WAITRESS AT the Dolphin, the restaurant across the street from Mrs. Duncan's rooming house, refilled Will's coffee cup, then Robert's. Will had taken the first flat he looked at in Toronto, a small attic in a red-brick house close to the lake in the west end. It had a bed frame with box springs and a mattress, linen, one wool blanket, a pillow, and a writing desk. The floor was covered with a worn shag carpet and the ceiling slanted down on both sides. There was one square window that had no screen and pushed open like a door. Will could stick his head out and look down to the lake. He loved the room the moment he saw it. The down sides were the bathroom and the kitchen; they both stank, the bathroom of urine because the toilet was temperamental about flushing, and the kitchen of coffee grounds and bananas. He didn't mind the smell of coffee, but the bananas bothered him.

Mrs. Duncan was an aged woman who, like the toilet, was temperamental. Upon greeting him on her doorstep, she had ushered him into the ground-floor parlour and served him tea and shortbread cookies. She detailed her rental policies to him: there were two rooms for rent, leaving five empty, seven boarders would be much too much for her, two kept her in tea and biscuits. All prospective tenants had to be clean, quiet and neat, which she could tell, she said, upon meeting them; there were to be no overnight guests; and, before concluding, she made a brief reference to her dead husband, ten years gone of a heart attack, damned cigarettes, which brought her to her final and most adamant point — no smoking in the house. Will agreed and gave her two months' rent on the spot even though he smoked a pack a day. He figured, if she couldn't smell the smoke on his clothes then it couldn't be that serious a request.

Robert Polski was Will's only friend in Parkdale. He looked about forty-five, but it was almost impossible to tell his age for sure because Robert lived on the street a good part of his time, even though he had a room at the Gladstone Hotel. He used it as an address, a place to pick up his mental disability benefits cheque. Robert saw a social worker once a week to make sure he was coping. He had wandered over to Will's booth at the Dolphin one morning and just started conversing. His first question was: "Do you want to buy these?" He had held out a bottle of his prescribed pills. Will read the label. It said Zolfax. Robert added that he was schizophrenic. "No," Will said, "but I would like to buy you breakfast," and that was how they had become friends.

"Are you still fasting?"

"I am," Will answered.

"But you drink coffee when you fast?"

"I do. It has no calories. There's just the accelerant and the diuretic. I have to be careful. Too much coffee and I could dehydrate myself."

Robert nodded. He had a Bible under his arm. Robert liked to read the Bible.

It was early, near 7:30 a.m. Will was getting up very early, which was unusual for him. He would take a shower in the foul-smelling bathroom — which was more bearable if he opened the window a crack, despite the chill of the spring mornings — then he'd tiptoe down the stairs, open the creaky front door slowly and slip out

"The way we live, these vicious money summits where tens of thousands of people show up to kick in windows and smash heads with cops? Where's the chaos coming from?"

"It's a separate investigation."

"I guess," Will said, and he flipped the edge of his paper back up. Will spoke from behind the paper. "Some cop got beat up a few blocks away last week. He's off duty and recovering at home. It says his jaw was broken in three places."

"Indians got him," Robert said.

Will pointed to Robert's Bible.

"Do you believe in the miracles, Robert?"

"I don't know. It's a separate study. Maybe Moses knew when the Red Sea would recede enough for them to cross. Maybe Moses was a a geophysicist, natural sciences, geophysics."

"So," Will said, "miracles might be undocumented science, then. Great insights without formula."

"Maybe a little like that," Robert said. "A little like that. The actual Bible is a fool's game, A fool's game. It could go on and on forever. It's chaos. A prophet could see and know."

"But where do they come from, Robert? What distinguishes them? Are we missing prophets because it's a simple case of misunderstanding? I mean, are prophets circumstantial? Are there certain circumstances that make them come into the world?"

Will put the paper down and leaned over the table.

"I mean, come on, think about it. There are parts of the rain forest in Costa Rica that have unique species based on a ten-foot difference in sea level. They have certain frogs and insects that only evolved to accommodate the specific moisture and consistent temperature of a specific altitude. If you go ten feet higher, or ten feet lower, these life forms can't survive. I mean, are prophets like that? Are they dependent on certain conditions in our environment, our economy, either really bad or really good, but nowhere in between? I'm trying to ask you here, Robert, if you've really thought about prophets?"

"Astrology," Robert said.

"What?"

"Astrology might be time's map, the map of time, bigger clocks, the stars and the planets. It might be a map of time, and if it's a map of time, then you can break it down, like seasons, and then you can, well, maybe you can know when the prophets bloom, or, maybe when they get seeded. IF the universe gets seeded with only so many prophets, then maybe, maybe then they're like frogs, like frogs in the imagination. Frogs die when the environment is too polluted, because they breathe through their skin."

"Possibly," Will said.

Dorothy walked up to the side of the booth with Robert's breakfast.

"Now you see," she said, looking at Will and pointing to the floor, "that's why we don't like him in here."

Will looked to the floor. There was a puddle of urine at Robert's feet.

"Oh, he'll be fine," Will said. He smiled at Dorothy.

"Fred says you have to have something to eat or you can't keep getting refills on your coffee."

"This one will be the last then," Will said. He held up his cup and smiled at Dorothy, who spun and walked away with the coffee pot. When she was out of earshot, Will turned to Robert and said, "Economists are the misbegotten progeny of prophets."

Robert's mouth hung open in bewilderment, a piece of egg falling to the plate.

A man appeared in front of their booth with a black duffel bag over his shoulder.

"You guys want smokes?" he asked.

Will asked the price, then bought a carton. It was an unbeatable price. The man wrote down his name — Cobb — and a cellphone number on a napkin and told Will to call him anytime he needed cigarettes. When Cobb left, Robert said, "That's my neighbour at the Gladstone."

SWEET GRASS

Cobb sat atop a garage roof. He looked over the gentle spring lake. The world was just beginning to take form. There were pink ribbons where the sky and the world met, a brightening of the darkness and the dimming of the few stars over the lake.

The garage was a four-car shed Cobb had rented on a side street in south Parkdale. It was well off the main road. It was the perfect place for his office and warehouse. Cobb had sold his first truck-load of cigarettes in three days. He kept his money in a small black bag under his bed. He had been out of prison a little over two weeks and had already made over eight thousand dollars.

Cobb looked in the direction of the hospital. There was a powerful medicine on the grounds. Cobb paid homage to the dead when he walked through the grounds at night, burned sweetgrass for the spirits on numerous occasions. He often left tobacco by the trees. The dead were powerful allies. The white man's people inside the hospital had no idea how much medicine there was on the ground.

Cobb had to report to his parole officer soon. By telephoning him from the reserve, he had put the first meeting off. He told Paddy Pape a story about his uncle dying, and that it was his wish and his uncle's wish that he be there for his passing. He told Paddy Pape that it could be any day. Paddy Pape was very sympathetic to his plight. There were no questions and there were no hassles. Cobb could stay with his uncle. Paddy Pape bartered well for the queen. Cobb knew he was going to have a good trading relationship with him.

Two headlights flashed in the pre-dawn darkness. Cobb spoke back with a flashlight. A white van found its way to Cobb's garage. Cobb climbed down off the roof and opened the garage door. Two Mohawks got out of the van and started unloading boxes of cigarettes into the garage. They unloaded the van in less than one minute. The two Mohawks waved quickly at Cobb, then got into the van and drove away just as quickly. Cobb closed the garage door and went back up onto the roof to finish watching the day's beginning. He burned sweet grass.

PRECIOUS

Cobb had been tracking his parole officer for a little over a week. He had to gather intelligence if his plan for freedom was going to work. Tracking was about two things, not losing a trail and not being seen. Cobb was a master of both. He used to track in Northern Ontario with his grandfather. They would disappear into the bush, leaving with nothing but a good knife and a flint stone. They could feed themselves, stay warm, and make shelter. They would return weeks later. City tracking was easier. Animals knew when they were being tracked. People rarely did. Paddy Pape had no idea he was being tracked. Cobb had a good file on Paddy.

People who knew Paddy Pape well called him Paddy Cake. He had come to Toronto from St. John's when he was a teenager, queer as a three dollar bill. He had tended bar, driven cab, and worked as a hustler. He obtained a degree in criminology, and since then he had been a parole officer. He spoke with only the slightest of Newfoundland tilts in his vowels, except when he was drunk, which was quite often, then it was pronounced. He took his job title quite seriously and viewed the world as a liberal penologist. Paddy's job was simple: tend to the dark sheep; keep them out of the queen's fields; keep them from blocking the queen's roads; and keep them from straining the queen's resources; and, if they didn't listen to him, put them back in prison.

Paddy Pape went to see Dr. Harry Wu twice a week. Wu was a reflexologist who had studied in Beijing then come to Canada. Paddy had cancer. He was dying. There was nothing Wu could do for him, except ease the pain. Paddy had refused chemotherapy. Wu had herbal remedies that could slow the cancer, even enduce a kind of inertia for a while, but sooner or later Paddy was going to die. Sooner or later everyone was going to die, but Paddy knew it more acutely than most, and it had changed his life completely.

At night, in his tiny bachelor apartment, Paddy would sometimes cry for periods as long as half an hour. Cobb couldn't figure out what brought on these crying spells. He broke into Paddy's apartment when Paddy was away. He did this numerous times. He was never seen. He never left anything out of place. He read journals and files. Paddy, like Cobb, kept detailed records. Paddy had been darting in and out of Randall's file, making margin notes in the margins of photocopies of the Queen's documents.

Parolee weeks out of prison...still hasn't made his first appointment.

Uncle sick and dying. Can't deny him the right to be with his family in a time of need.

Cobb knew Paddy had the right, by law, to demand that he, the parolee, appear for a scheduled meeting. He had the right to issue a warrant for the parolee. He had the right to send him back to Warkworth. Paddy had the right to do many things. The queen had vested a portion of her power in Paddy Pape.

Parolee promised he would make an appearance before 1 p.m. on Sunday.

The journals were more informal. These were Paddy's personal notes. They were a kind of outline for dealing with Randall. Cobb was touched by the journal. Paddy truly cared.

Randall Seymour has to be one of the most hideous monsters of a human being I've seen in quite a while. He stands six-foot-two and weighs 245 pounds. He has eyes darker than midnight, not a hint of feeling in the face, not a line to be read, no path to the man. He looks like a savage. The eyes pierce rather than speak.

Cobb had watched Paddy sit and stare at his picture for long periods of time. The notes amused him because they told Cobb what Paddy thought when he looked at his picture.

A hard case. Should be with Aboriginal service? Shouldn't an Indian be doing this?

Randall chuckled when he read that. He was a hard case.

No point disputing the file with Correctional Services. They gave it to me, and I have given my life to providence. There has to be a reason this Indian has come to me.

That line moved Randall quite a bit. He thought about it for a few minutes. He was particularly moved by Paddy's surrender to the Great Spirit.

Cobb was not surprised by the basic biographical information.

Randall Seymour is twenty-eight. He has no sisters and no brothers. He was orphaned by a mother who died while sniffing gasoline. She popped pills and drank rubbing alcohol. Her body was a mess. They found her in a hotel in Parkdale the year Randall turned sixteen. She left the reserve the year he was born, left him in the care of Indians.

An arrest history the consistency of a menstrual cycle. Always destruction of property. Frequently charges stayed without consideration to the Crown's duty to protect property.

Of course Paddy was right. The queen had to protect the property of her subjects and, for reasons never quite detailed in the psychology reports, Randall had taken to the destruction of property, just wanton destruction with no profit motive. That ended, though, in his early twenties.

Probably when he settled into smuggling cigarettes. Many criminals take a long time to find their niche.

First significant detention was the result of blowing up a small police trailer in northern Ontario. It had been used by the Ontario Provincial Police.

The thing that was notable about it to Paddy was the construction of the bomb. It showed real intelligence. Randall had made a bomb out of gasoline, petroleum jelly, ball bearings, metal shards, surrounded by an air pocket that filled with vapor from the way the gasoline mixed with the Vaseline, making it much more powerful in its initial expansion, thus propelling the ball bearings and the metal shards at a much higher velocity than a simple gasoline bomb. It was detonated with a piece of sandpaper attached to the vapour chamber, to prevent it from getting wet, and surrounded by match heads that were set into motion with a remote control taken from a child's toy.

The OPP had thought they were dealing with an eco-terrorist. Their forensics people were worried by the sophistication of the bomb. It wasn't the kind of ordnance they usually saw in their policing duties, the lab guy had written in his report, and Paddy had underlined it. The trailer had been completely destroyed. They never would have caught Randall, but for the fact that he came back the next day to look at the damage and to make notes. He mistakenly brought the same notebook that contained his original design for the bomb: ratios, weights, volume, all the detail of a military specification.

Seymour's whole file speaks of a kind of unfocused determination, the cry of a misdirected intelligence. I'm going to help this one. I'm going to direct that intelligence toward the benefit of humanity, his own fulfillment. He must want to fit in positively and constructively, to see his acute cunning, mental discipline, and perseverance go to the betterment of the human species. He needs to realize how precious his life is.

That one word, "precious," told Cobb everything he needed to know. Paddy Pape wanted to work on a difficult case before he left the world.

Paddy had a large dog. Every time Cobb broke into Paddy's apartment he brought a treat for the dog, who adapted to the situation like any opportunist, taking the treat and going into a corner to eat it or chew on it. By the third break-in the dog had stopped growling. It recognized Cobb's smell.

The second part of Cobb's agenda was to know the man who was trying to know him. His journals were full of Paddy's reflections on life and death. They began only ten months earlier, probably when Paddy was diagnosed. Paddy's mind had wandered back to the child he once was. Every day was new and every night he fell asleep with deep gratitude and love for the day he had lived. A deeper and deeper sense of wonderment was taking hold of him. His mind often followed sounds on the street into some kind of stupor, a kind of a trance. Life hypnotized him. He wanted desperately to maintain the deepest possible connection he could with the world, and the prospect of death was teaching him that compassion was the only real way to live. Cobb liked Paddy.

In the end it wasn't the semen that got him, and that was a miracle in itself. Paddy had been having unprotected sex for years. Most of his sex partners were transients of one sort or another, people in motion, the occasional parolee, wherever he could find a cock. In the last two decades of his life, he couldn't recall a relationship that had gone longer than six weeks. Paddy had been in love once. He was thirty-four when it began. He was thirty-five when it ended. That was twenty years before. The man he loved went back to his wife. In some part of his mind he had always figured he would get AIDS. Since being diagnosed with cancer he had thought often about his sex life, and he had been forced to wonder if it wasn't some death wish he had carried in his heart all those years, some contempt for whatever made him, and some contempt for the forces of nature that shaped his wants and then told them he shouldn't have them. The cancer had been very good for Paddy.

Parkdale was good for the kind of reckless sex Paddy craved. He liked to suck. He didn't crave reciprocal behaviour. The sated man would leave and Paddy would masturbate, alone. Cobb had seen four men go into his apartment in the nine days he had been tracking Paddy.

Cancer was a human disease. AIDS was a fag disease. The difference was immeasurable. Paddy was grateful for the cancer, and grateful for the dignity of dying like a human being and not a fag. Since he'd found out he was dying he had sucked all the cock he could get.

The weather was warm for spring, and Paddy walked past buildings and people he had seen for years. He was going to die in this community, and he was going to die alone. That was part of the reason he had chosen reflexology for his end-of-life medical treatment. A parolee he had know some years back had studied it with a prison volunteer, spoken very highly of it, a way to balance body and mind. It was all in Paddy's personal journals. It was amazing to Cobb what a man dying alone put to paper. It was a message in a bottle. Cobb found it.

Cobb watched Paddy go into Wu's clinic. Paddy wrote in his personal journals that Dr. Wu was doing something to him, that some energy point in his body had been opened, something he hadn't been able to find with any of his own resources and which caused the nearly euphoric state that coincided with his approaching death. When he had first started going for his sessions with Dr. Wu, horrible bruises would appear on Paddy's body, and each encounter was painful, but now they were a joy. He looked forward to the sessions with Dr. Wu, and he always left in a bit of a daze, almost like being drunk, but with no loss of motor skills.

On this particular day, the session was quite effective. Cobb watched Paddy walk home slowly and in complete serenity. Paddy stopped at an ATM on the way and withdrew some money. When Paddy looked at the transaction record, the balance on his account mystified him. Cobb watched his reactions closely. The spider had taken the fly.

SUPERNOVA

WILLIAM TOBE OFTEN WENT for long walks. He had read that walking was a meditation and, as he had no job, he needed something to do. He had not held a job in his life, so he had absolutely no idea what it was like. He had worked very hard in his short life. If he had not taken this time off he would be in law school in the fall. If he studied in the summers, he would be a lawyer before he was twenty-three. In his dormitory at the University of Ottawa, it hadn't occurred to him that time off from school and family to pursue a vision would require some structure. If he wanted to maintain his sanity. He did. So he structured his life.

The walks could go on for hours. While walking, he would recite prayers from his childhood — the Lord's Prayer, or sometimes one of Milarepa's one hundred thousand songs, of which he had memorized many. Sometimes he would recite sections from Lao Tsu's verses or Chuang Tsu. Were he thinking in academic terms, he would have realized he was comparing religions, but he wasn't thinking in academic terms. He was just structuring his days and trying to make sense of what he believed was a vision.

Will walked into the donut shop, got a donut and a coffee and found a table in the back. He pulled out the envelope he'd put in his pocket that morning — it had been waiting for him in the vestibule — but before he could start to read the letter he had to address a lady. She was giving him a look he had become accustomed to in the neighbourhood. It was a death look, a direct and unblinking gaze that locked onto him. The person who owned the gaze was an old woman with black hair streaked with grey and a wrinkled, prune-like face. He knew the moment he locked onto her that he'd be dreaming about her. They always came to him in his dreams, the ones that gave him the death look. This woman was trying to make a withdrawal from him. The people in the neighbourhood tried to take anything they could from him, even emotional sustenance. He didn't mind it as much as being asked for change all the time. They had taught him one of the fundamental rules of economics: need has a power of its own.

The power of this old woman's need was overwhelming. Will felt assaulted, but there was nothing he could do. All space is violated under overwhelming need. Any kind of property is communal when need is overwhelming. Her eyes were black and piercing. Her inner world had collapsed.

He had nothing for her, and he felt guilty for not having anything he could show through his eyes that she might feel for a moment, but there wasn't a cent of compassion in him.

She broke her stare, stood up and left the donut shop.

He returned to his coffee and his letter, which was from his sister in New York. He had given her his address in Toronto. His thoughts were interrupted a moment or two later by Persephone Bluette, whom he had known but forgotten. "Is this seat taken?" She pointed to the one other seat at his table.

Will took a quick look around. There were no other seats. He said it was not. He had to be awake in that neighbourhood. Persey said she didn't think the streetcar would be around for a while, so she had decided to have a coffee. He still didn't recognize her. He guessed that she was about twenty, but she groomed herself, at least when she went to work at the hospital, like a middle-aged woman. She pulled her hair back in a chignon, which made her face very austere. It was the first thing he noticed. After he took a good look at her, he decided that she was beautiful, but not in a model-like way. No, she was just beautiful — demure, good skin, delicate features. She said that she hoped she wasn't disturbing him. He thought that was pretty decent, but a little stupid because what would she have done if he had said she was?

So he said, "No, not at all, please sit down."

Then she said, "You look very familiar."

He told her he was in the donut shop quite a bit. She said that wasn't it, that she was sure she knew him from somewhere else. The first thing that came to his mind was university, so he asked her if she had ever lived in Ottawa. She had, and it turned out that they had both gone to the University of Ottawa. She remembered that they took the same second year humanities elective, sociology, and were in the same section. She said she remembered him because he was the only one in the class that looked as young as her. He had started university when he was sixteen, had skipped a couple of grades, he told her. So had she. In fact they'd both skipped the second grade. He asked her what she thought they might have missed and she thought that was really funny. She said, "what we might have missed" three or four times and laughed each time. That was the only thing she laughed about. The rest of the time she was intensely calm.

They introduced themselves. She was Persey, short for Persephone, and he was Will, short for William. She spoke quickly and succinctly, never hesitating or pausing, like she'd written down what she was going to say. She asked him what he was doing then and he said, "Just hanging out."

She said, "No, not this instant, in general."

He said, "Yeah, I know. Just hanging out."

"Are you going to school?"

"No."

She glanced around the donut shop, then she leaned in a little closer to him. "That woman that left just before I sat down is my ward."

"Excuse me?" Will said.

"That old woman. She's been court-ordered to psychiatric evaluation. She stabbed a courier in her front hall."

Will winced. "Did she kill him?"

"No. He's fine. The blade only went in a quarter of an inch."

"Why did she do it?" Will asked.

"We don't know yet."

Will nodded.

Persey told him that she had been accepted into graduate studies that commenced in the fall. She was doing a co-op at the mental health centre. Will asked her if she knew anything about schizophrenia. He had spoken at length with Robert Polski about it at the Dolphin, and Robert had told him that they didn't have a clue what it was. They knew the characteristics, Robert had told him. They could tell the characteristics, but they couldn't define the disease.

She told Will that little was really known but it was a great topic for a thesis. She couldn't quite believe that he was doing nothing, so he told her he was interpreting a vision.

She didn't blink an eye. She just said, "unh-huh."

Will saw the scars on Persey's wrists when she was holding her coffee mug with both hands. It couldn't have been much past six months since she'd tried to kill herself, going by the tender look to the skin. He was dumbfounded by the scars. The idea of Persey trying to kill herself was horrifying to him. She seemed so valuable somehow, but he couldn't think of how. It just made him sad that she had ever wanted to die.

"What are the characteristics of a vision?" she asked.

"My vision or a vision? I would think you more qualified to answer the latter."

"I deal with delusions and hallucinations," she said, and she used those words like she had no doubts about what they meant.

"Well, if you don't know what a vision is, how do you know the difference between a delusion and a vision?" he asked her.

She stared out the window for a couple of seconds, then at him, then she started to speak at length. Will would later think that the first few questions were just some kind of test. She told him all about her co-op at the hospital.

The hospital was eerie in its quiet. Early in the morning was one of those times, just before the loons woke up and remembered they were insane. They could forget they were insane when they slept, she claimed. "Everyone is sane when they sleep," Persey said. She told him that the human interior could not be understood. It was the great humbling they all went through. Doctors did the best they could. It didn't matter how many ways they devised to see activity in the brain, they would never understand it. She qualified her position as realistic, not cynical. Will nodded his head. He was just happy for the conversation. He knew nothing about mental health. Persey went on with her debriefing, and that was how he characterized it later, when he was walking home, a debriefing. It was like she had been sitting on all this stuff, just waiting for an opportunity to unload it all, and Will was the person she chose. He later came to the conclusion that it was their common life experience that allowed her to unload her stress and grief. How many times do you bump into someone randomly who has that much in common with you? It was all reasonable. He could understand it.

The feelings she had walking the hospital halls at night were overwhelming. It was her first exposure to the workings of this kind of an institution. She thought she was going to have a nervous breakdown. She couldn't look the patients in their eyes. There was no relationship between them. So many of them were court-ordered. The whole thing was fuelled on expedience and the continuous deferral of the liability involved in making a decision. In lieu of a decision, the staff was allowed to observe, and they were allowed to recommend further observation by other observers in other places. They could keep a person in the system for weeks or months without having to account for their actions, and say, "we don't know" at the end of it all. Will wondered why she was working in the mental health field if she didn't like it. It was her mother's profession. Persey's mother was one of the most respected psychiatrists in Toronto, a leader in the field of premenstrual syndrome, with a small portion of her practice devoted to counselling as a condition of parole. Those were the patients her mother liked the best. She felt like she was really doing something when she worked with the lost souls who found themselves in the Canadian justice system.

Persey, however, was having some kind of reaction to the profession. She had begun to wonder if pure research might not be a better choice for her. She was still young and, perhaps she concluded, her concerns were just some childish concessions she had made to her heart that now had to be released. It was probably all just part of growing up, but still, the feelings she had walking those halls at night ... There was so much suffering. Every kind of pain known to humankind was on display. It was very humbling.

She had been away from the University of Ottawa a while. Her mother had charted her summer: extracurricular work for future application forms. Persey was monitoring the effects of a new drug three days a week.

Persey worked on the trials of Zolfax, a drug that stopped outbursts, certain forms of mania in schizophrenics. It worked. It worked just fine. The problem was that it didn't do anything to heal the affliction. In fact, so much of mental health was just a stop-gap solution. Drug therapy was a never-ending revenue stream for pharmaceutical companies and health-care professionals.

Persey was not overwhelmed with disgust or self-loathing, or any other feeling of defeat, by these realizations. The patients needed respite from their suffering. It was just that sometimes it seemed a great injustice could be happening. But she had no proof.

Mrs. Rabini, the woman who had left the donut shop after staring through Will for a few minutes, was her main study in the extracurricular work she was doing at the institution. The hospital had made room for Persey because her mother had made inquiries at the highest levels, and because Persey came for free, and her work would be turned over to Zolfax's parent company, where it would be mined for the rhetoric to fill the government forms that regulated their industry.

Mrs. Rabini's case history was interesting. She had started to clean her home in the middle of the night. Her husband had thought this behaviour was a little strange and he asked her not to do it. Still, he would wake up to the sound of the vacuum cleaner downstairs at 3 a.m. The Rabini's three children were grown and no longer lived at home. Mr. Rabini's first thought on his wife's strange behaviour was that she had been deeply affected by the engagement of their youngest child, and had started to express this in her odd practices. Mr. Rabini had asked his eldest son, Franco, to speak to his mother. Franco had come over and drunk coffee and eaten cake his mother put on the table. He'd asked her about the late night cleaning. She'd said that the place was always a mess. He'd asked nothing more. He'd told his father he would probably just have to live with it. "She's going to keep doing it, Pop." Mr. Rabini had shrugged his shoulders and rolled his eyes. When Mrs. Rabini refused to go to her daughter's wedding, because the house was a mess, a terrible argument had broken out. Mr. Rabini had gone to the wedding and reception by himself — in his immaculately pressed shirt and fifteen-year-old suit. When his daughter did not see her mother she threatened to cancel the wedding. Mr. Rabini, having paid the caterer already, would not hear of it. His daughter and wife had stopped speaking from that day on.

All of this, however, had not landed Mrs. Rabini under twenty-four hour supervision at the Queen Street Addiction and Mental Health Hospital as a Zolfax guinea pig. No, what landed Mrs. Rabini under supervision was the aforementioned courier who stepped into her front hall one Wednesday morning without shaking off his boots and, thus, dropping a pile of slush on the acrylic runner that had sat on the floor in front of the door for eight years, he was sent to the hospital with a puncture wound to his abdomen. The doctor had told him his assailant was good with a knife and had not wanted to kill him, only wound him. He'd asked the young courier if the assailant had held the knife at the top of the blade. The courier told the doctor that she had not, that she had held it at the handle. The doctor had frowned and told the young man he had been very lucky.

"Geez," Will interjected. "It's amazing what a thread we all hang by."

Persey looked him square in the eye, as though her core message had been received by another, and she nodded her head.

Mrs. Rabini had stayed in her room for most of her two weeks at the hospital. She was due to be released in sixteen days. Mrs. Rabini had been diagnosed with a kind of dementia that was broad, but perfect for Zolfax. Under the medication, she had not tried to clean the hospital. In her family sessions with Persey and a senior physician at the hospital, she showed some awareness of how strange her behaviour had been. The drug was effective and there were no impediments to her release. She would be prescribed Zolfax and it would cost her family about $600 a month. The prescription would be lifted when there was enough evidence that the ailment, never cured, never really defined, passed on its own.

Persey took a big gulp of her coffee and then the first significant silence since she began talking settled in around them.

Will said, "Do you believe in God?"

Persey furrowed her brow and looked at him like he was an alien. She didn't say a word.

"I think God's an economist," Will said.

CRUCIFIX

A SOFT PALE LIGHT slipped through the small square window and spilled into the attic of Mrs. Duncan's rooming house. Will had to get around to putting the mattress on the floor. He hated the bed frame. It was as ancient as her. He didn't mind sleeping on the floor. There were no mice and no cockroaches. He had grown used to the smell of urine in the bathroom and the smell of coffee and bananas in the kitchen.

It was dark and damp outside.

Rain is like memory, he thought. Memory is despicable. The past should die easily. He needed some breakfast. Or should he continue the fast, he wondered. The holy types fasted. He had to get out of his room, leave the window. He moved quietly past the dull green and white wallpaper. The stairs creaked. It was hard to be quiet. The kitchen had an east-facing widow. He crept down the hall, intent on a morning walk along the lake.

"Mr. Tobe," Mrs. Duncan said from the door to the parlour that she opened quickly, surprising him.

"Oh, hello. You're up early, Mrs. Duncan."

"As are you, Mr. Tobe."

"Yes. I was going to take my morning walk."

"A morning constitutional is good for your serenity."

"Yes. I like to start my day with them."

"Would you like a cup of tea and a cookie?"

"Tea would be nice, thank you."

"Come in."

She prepared the tea.

"Milk, sugar, honey, Mr. Tobe?"

"Earl Grey, Mrs. Duncan?"

"Yes."

"Just honey, thank you. May I help you?"

"Oh, no. That's quite nice of you, Mr. Tobe. I can manage."

She was being kind to him. He didn't want to cause her any distress. He would have to stop smoking in his room.

"Well, there you are."

"Thank you."

"You're quite welcome. Do you go to mass, Mr. Tobe?"

"Please, call me Will."

"Will."

"No. I've slipped from the church, Mrs. Duncan. I was taken as a child, but as a teenager I was given a choice to attend or not. My mother almost became a nun before she married."

That lit her up. He felt good, making her feel good.

"You're very fortunate to come from such good stock, Will."

"My mother and father met before she went into the convent. After a year she realized a family was her true calling."

"It's a very high calling. Only the chosen survive, Will."

"A very disciplined life, my mother always said."

"She sounds like a wonderful woman."

"Thank you. She is."

"I wonder if you would like to attend mass with me this morning, Will?"

"Thank you. That's very kind, but no."

"We have a wonderful new priest, a young man like yourself.

He's full of insight into your generation. I think he could bring you back to the church."

"I don't know, Mrs. Duncan."

"It's just up the street. We could walk. I would so enjoy it if you'd come with me."

"Okay."

"Wonderful. We should leave right after our tea. It would please your mother, I'm sure, if you were to call her and tell her you had attended mass."

Will said that he would call her, but he had no intention of following through. Mrs. Duncan buttoned up her jacket. When she was finished, Will opened the door and they stepped out into the Sunday morning. Across the street, there was a child blowing soap bubbles. Mrs. Duncan let it be known she felt it was inappropriate to leave children unattended in their community.

On the way to church Will saw Cobb out of the corner of his eye. He was slipping into the Dolphin with a black duffel bag over his shoulder. Will remembered he needed more smokes.

INTERPRETATION

WILL SPOKE FROM BEHIND the newspaper. Robert was on the other side of the paper, on the other side of the booth.

"You see, it's all a matter of interpretation. That's what the point of it is, just interpretation. I mean, if I were to say that Moses was an economist, you might think I was crazy, completely mental —"

"I don't think you're crazy," Robert said.

"Thanks, Robert, but what I meant is that it's just a question of interpretation. You could say that the ten commandments are the foundation for an economy, because an economy is an organized and just community, and the principle of organization is trust. How can you trust an adulterer, a thief, a liar? Once those things are in place you have the basis of a contract, a social contract, and contracts are the basis of an economy."

Dorothy, the waitress at the Dolphin, arrived at their booth. It was a Wednesday morning, eleven o'clock.

"He can't piss himself today," she said.

"He's not going to piss himself," Will said.

"The usual?" she asked.

"Yes," Will said.

He watched her walk away.

"If there were no contracts there could be no modern world, no world whatsoever. It's the contract that acts as the binding agent."

"Faith is a contract," Robert said. "Faith is a contract."

"Yes it is," Will said. "Faith is a very important contract. People have to have faith in one another for the contracts to hold. When I say Moses was an economist I mean that he was a nation builder. He could set his people in a place, and in a spirit, with the promise of milk and honey. They believed him. They really believed him. That's the problem."

"What's the problem?" Robert asked.

"There's nothing left to believe."

Dorothy returned to fill Robert's and Will's cups. She left four creamers on the table, not too rudely. She wasn't mean. It was just that she had to clean up the mess that Robert always made. When she saw nothing, she turned and walked away.

Will looked at Robert.

"There's no belief anymore. There's no great story. People watch TV now and they see a guy in a suit trying to sell them something. There's nothing to believe anymore. They just don't get it. What is a Minister of Oceans and Fisheries going to do when the Deputy Minister tells him there's no more cod in the Atlantic, that it's been overfished. And he's been told by the research directors, who have been told by the guys in the rubber suits who dive under the water and do the tests, and then the Minister of Oceans and Fisheries tells the Prime Minister and then he has to announce a moratorium on fishing. Then everyone wants to know why their elected official can't make more fish. It's insane, Robert, insane. We were better off with kings, Robert. Equality is going to destroy us, but, like I said, it's all a matter of interpretation, if you can believe Moses was an economist.

"Everything that grows has to die. It's the natural cycle. We talk of the economy growing, but the economy proper can never die. We speak about it in organic terms — growth in the economy — but we never speak about the inevitable consequence of growth, which is, of course, death. Fractional reserve banking has committed us to never-ending growth, otherwise the money caves in on itself, massive devaluation. To grow we acquire debt by borrowing from the banks. Our government does this for us. To pay the debt, they tax us. To continue the growth of the economy, which has to happen to keep the currency values, we have to produce more and more, and in producing more and more, we consume more and more."

Dorothy appeared with Robert's food and placed it on the table in front of him.

Robert started eating. Will spoke from behind the paper.

"Every time the dollar goes up, exports go down. This government wants a low dollar. They don't have any vision. There's just so many holes, Robert, so many holes in the economy. It sure isn't Moses. No matter how you interpret it."

Will looked out from behind his paper. Robert had finished his eggs and was humming to the wall.

"Economics is our fundamental communication," Will said. "What language does a prophet speak, Robert?"

"The language before words."

"How could there be a language before words?"

"Words are just an interpretation. A tree is a tree. It's the thing itself. The word tree is artificial in our language, and it's artificial in every language."

Will let the paper fall. He stared at Robert, mouth agape. Dorothy returned to the table and handed him the bill. Will reached into his pocket. It was a conditioned reflex. Dorothy spoke a silent language. The bill meant she wanted them to leave. She had taken a business-only policy with Robert. She didn't like him staying too long after he finished eating. He scared away customers.

"Unh, excuse me," Will said to Dorothy. "I forgot my money. Do you mind if I go home to get it."

"You can't leave without paying."

"I live just across the street."

"You can't leave without paying," she said again.

"No faith," Robert said.

"It's policy. No credit. No personal cheques." She was red in the face when she said this.

"I'll get it," said a voice from the next booth. Will turned around to see Cobb, who stood. He picked up the bill, handed it back to Dorothy with a ten dollar bill. She left immediately.

"I'm not a bum," Will said.

"I guess that's a matter of interpretation," Cobb said.

"She hates me," Robert said.

Cobb looked at Robert and Will.

"You guys good for smokes?"

"I don't get my benefits cheque until Friday."

"I'll trade you a carton for some pills," Cobb said. "It's easy to sell medicine."

"Okay," Robert said, and handed Cobb a plastic prescription bottle. Cobb handed him a carton of smokes.

"You good, Will?"

"Yes."

"You owe me ten bucks," Cobb said to Will. Then he leaned in close to Will's ear and said, "People like us have to stick together."

With that statement he departed.

BOY

THERE WAS A KNOCK at Paddy Pape's door. He awoke on the loveseat in his bachelor apartment. Some of the candles had burnt out. The clock on the wall said 11:55. It was five minutes to a new day, a Wednesday, if his mind was clear. He had passed out. He struggled to put the evening back together in his mind. Who could that be at the door? He got up and felt something wet on his stomach. He remembered masturbating. Shortly after dinner, pan-fried bratwurst with onions and mustard, a bag of chips, a lot of rye. He must have fallen asleep, drunk.

"Just a minute," Paddy said. He walked into the bathroom where he grabbed a hand towel and wiped his stomach. Part of the semen had dried and he would have to wait until his morning shower to clean it off. It was stuffy in the little basement apartment. He splashed water on his face then slipped into his pink housecoat and walked to the door.

"Yes," he said, opening the door, with a touch of anger in his voice, an anger that completely softened when he saw what was before him. It was a boy.

Cobb was at the end of the hall, tucked around a corner. He could hear the boy and he could hear Paddy. Cobb had been keeping watch on Paddy for the entire evening, peering into the small basement window every few minutes, waiting for the best time to begin his operation.

"I need a place," the boy said.

"I beg your pardon?"

"I need a place to stay."

"Do I know you?"

King, Paddy's devoted dog, stood at his side, with both ears pricked up, wondering when Cobb was going to pop into the scene with a treat, as the dog could smell Cobb out the door and down the hall. King was a formidable sight, some kind of Rottweiler mix.

The boy looked at King and then he looked at Paddy. He spoke softly.

"I was told I could crash on your sofa."

"Who said that?"

"People in the neighbourhood said you sometimes do favours. They said I could trust you."

"What's your name?"

"Michael."

"How old are you?"

"Eighteen."

"Where are you from?"

"Halifax."

"How long have you been on the streets?"

"Six weeks."

"Why do you need a place to stay tonight?"

"I just got a problem, you know. I can't be seen around tonight. I owe some people some stuff, you know, and I need a place to stay, just for tonight, then I'm going back to Halifax tomorrow, hitchhiking. They said you would help."

"They were right, Michael from Halifax."

The boy walked in and Paddy closed the door behind him. Cobb bolted up the stairs, out the front door, and around the side of the building to the small window that peered into Paddy's bachelor apartment.

AUTHORITY

PERSEY WAS NO LESS talkative the next time she and Will met. It was a chance meeting at the same donut shop. She walked in and sat down with her coffee as though Will should have been expecting her. He was happy to see her. He lowered his Sunday newspaper and smiled. There were a few pleasantries, then she did exactly what she had the first time they met; she divested herself of malignant psychic energy, as though he were her therapist. She was returning from a visit to the hospital.

That day, he learned that Persey had no father. She had been created by her mother and her mother alone. She had no brothers and no sisters. Her mother, one of the first women to plow her way through the male-dominated faculty of medicine at the University of Toronto, had decided in her early forties, after ten years of medical practice and research, to produce an heir. Persey was heir to Dr. Irene Bluette's legacy of research and good standing in the fields of premenstrual stress and convict counselling. She was being groomed like a racehorse and, in fact, her conception was not unlike that of a racehorse's. Her father, the stud, as Persey referred to him, had been selected from a genius sperm pool. Her mother had taken eighteen months to make up her mind. She finally settled on the semen of a Russian physicist, whose name Persey did not know, as her mother felt that knowing her father, beyond his field, titles, awards and general genetic makeup, was pointless. After all, Persey had her, a loving mother who devoted herself to her work and her daughter. What more could Persey want?

Will also got an update on Mrs. Rabini. Persey had seen her that morning and she had noticed that Mrs. Rabini had a look of grace, as though some secret had been given to her and her alone. She'd sat on the bed, already dressed with her hair back. Her face had looked younger. She'd had her hands folded on her lap, and she was rocking gently back and forth on the bed, humming a song to herself. Persey had stared through the small glass square in her door for a while before entering the room, wondering why Mrs. Rabini looked so good.

Persey had asked Mrs. Rabini how she was. Mrs. Rabini had told her she was fine. Persey had brought her medicine and she had put it down on the small stand beside the bed. As Persey had reached for the water and paper cup with the Zolfax in it, the white smock she wore to signify her membership in the auspicious collective of healers, experimenters and general practitioners had pulled up at the sleeves, revealing two scars, a half-dime each in width, running parallel with her forearms and an inch-and-a-half long. It was the first time she had been so careless at the hospital as to allow her suicide attempt to be seen by a patient. Their eyes had locked for a long moment before Persey had broken the spell and spoke, an act which commands attention when you wear a lab smock in an institution.

Dr. Singh had told Mrs. Rabini that she would be going home at the end of the week, so Mrs. Rabini smiled every morning, rocking on the bed as she washed down the pill. Mrs. Rabini had stopped rocking and had looked at Persey. The smile on her face had shut down like a storefront at closing time.

A thin sheen of perspiration glossed Persey's forehead. It was downhill from there. She had been slow and shaky standing up. She'd thought Mrs. Rabini was going to attempt to help her. Anger had welled in her. She'd composed herself and looked sternly, but without malice, at Mrs. Rabini. Her look had said, I'm the boss here. I'm the one who helps patients who have lost their balance. Not a single word was passed.

Persey had maintained her gaze on Mrs. Rabini and told her to get her breakfast. The cafeteria would be open in fifteen minutes. She'd told Mrs. Rabini she would stop by later to give her her second pill and to talk with her. She'd admonished Mrs. Rabini not to forget that her husband would be there in the afternoon.

As Persey had walked down the hall, it had occurred to her that the anxiety she'd just felt was one of the biggest emotions she'd experienced in some time, and she'd wondered if fear and anxiety were a dream of sorts, a dream without pictures.

When she was finished she took her customary pause, sipped her coffee, and allowed Will to speak into the silence.

None of this protocol had been explained to Will. He just intuited it.

"Why did you try to kill yourself?" he asked.

She stared at him for a few seconds then started to cry.

PEACE PIPE

COBB WALKED ALONG THE street. It was close to noon on Sunday. He had to make his first appearance at his parole officer's place, or risk having a warrant issued for his arrest. Forms had to be filled out. A folder had to be started. Reports had to be filed. The queen wanted to keep watch over Cobb. Cobb had told Paddy that his only remaining blood relative, Elmer, was dying of a bacterial infection in his bowels. The only concern on Elmer's mind was his desire to sell more contraband cigarettes so he could get a new motor for the boat he used to over-fish the lakes in the spring — not his own lake of course, the cottagers' lakes — but Paddy didn't need to know that.

A police cruiser passed. Cobb kept his eyes low to the ground. A man stumbled out of the alley right in front of Cobb. He had to stop or he would have run right into him. It was Robert Polski, who had just woken from a nap.

"Hey, Cobb," Robert said.

"Hey Robert. Come by my room tomorrow. I have some forms to fill out with you."

"Those the ones, the ones you give a free carton of smokes for?"

"Yep."

"What time?"

"Any time after six in the evening."

"Okay."

Cobb moved on, down the street, under the street lamps, past the parked cars, the lit windows of donut shops, dollar stores, medical clinics, legal-aid offices and apartments. He turned left onto a small side street and scanned the house numbers. Some of the houses were still family dwellings. Some were rooming houses and some had been converted to multiple apartments.

Young William Tobe was across the street, pacing in the parking lot, smoking a cigarette, talking to himself. Cobb walked across the front lawn of one of the larger houses. He descended a half-flight of stairs, into a hallway with a single light bulb illuminating it. He knocked on door number B2.

"Yes?" a voice asked.

"Randall Seymour," he said.

The door flew open and a man stood there, smiling, holding a drink and a cigarette in the same hand.

"Paddy Pape," he said. "Please come in."

Cobb walked into the little bachelor apartment. King stood and stared at Cobb. The dog was very protective, Cobb noted. He had to deal with the dog before he dealt with Paddy Pape.

Cobb sat down.

"Well, now, Randall, would you like a drink?"

"No."

"Would you like to smoke a joint?"

"Okay."

"Great. I want us to be comfortable. I guess that you're used to the types in the correctional services industry, but I like to be a little less formal. I want us to be friends. If we can't be friends then I can't help you."

"Yep."

Paddy lit a joint and passed it to Cobb.

"I'm here to help you readjust to society and you're here to help me think that I'm doing my job."

"Okay."

"Excellent. This is an excellent start. I think this is going to go really well. Now, the first thing we have to address is this job we have for you. They were expecting you weeks ago, but I told them about your uncle and, with a little pleading on my part, they agreed to wait for you rather than hire someone else. So the first commitment I need from you, Randall, is that you will show up to work tomorrow. Can you give me that commitment?"

"Listen," Cobb said. "I have nothing against you. This isn't personal."

Cobb pulled out a yellow envelope from the back pocket of his jeans. He threw it down on the dirty coffee table. Paddy picked up the envelope and pulled out a few pictures: Paddy fellating the boy, Michael, who had wandered into his life, according to his story, and another of Paddy penetrating Michael. Cobb knew he hadn't done that in a long time.

"And more like them," Cobb said.

"Listen, I can put you right back in for this, Randall. This is ridiculous. That was between Michael and me. This has nothing to do with your parole. What were you doing outside my window anyway? How did you know?"

Cobb reached back into his pocket and pulled out a sheet of white paper. He unfolded it slowly and placed it on the table in front of Paddy. It was a photocopy of a phony birth certificate Cobb had manufactured at a copy shop. It said Michael was born in the Halifax General Hospital, and that he was fifteen.

"He's just shy of sixteen," Cobb said.

"Oh, Christ," Paddy said, and he started to cry.

"Take it easy."

"He told me he was eighteen."

"You got a transcript?"

"You miserable cocksucker."

"It takes one to know one."

"It's not illegal," Paddy said.

"If you just blew him, no, but the anal intercourse is illegal under the age of eighteen."

"That's horseshit," Paddy said. His eyes were full of water and he was sniffling.

Cobb pulled out another piece of paper, a photocopy, the product of his research at the library. The white man's world wasn't so bad when it worked for him. He read aloud: "The Criminal Code of Canada, section 159: Every person who engages in an act of anal intercourse is guilty of an indictable offence and liable to imprisonment for a term not exceeding ten years or is guilty of an offence punishable on summary conviction, except: subsection one does not apply to any act engaged in, in private, between husband and wife, or any two persons, each of whom is eighteen years of age or more, both of whom consent to the act. For the purposes of subsection —"

"What?" Paddy said.

"Now you can go to court and see what the Crown makes of all this, and, yeah, I'm a parolee, and, yeah, I'm blackmailing you, and for sure I'll go back in — but, brother, there's still this stuff, and there's still the boy himself, and I can get him any time I need him, and he can testify, so, yeah, you can take this all to the Crown if you want, but, brother, the queen and her agents, they're not like you."

"You pimped that boy to me."

"No. He does what he did with you for a living. I paid him. I didn't make him what he is."

Paddy sniffled. "What do you want?"

"Freedom."

"You've been paroled."

"I want to be free."

"I understand," Paddy said. "You don't want someone climbing up your ass."

"I had twelve thousand dollars wired into your bank account. I want us to be friends. I'm going to need friends if I'm going to survive here."

"That was you, the twelve thousand? I could have you sent back for trying to bribe your parole officer."

"Medicine is expensive. I know that you're sick, Paddy. I gave you the money to help you and I don't want a forced contract with you. I can turn the pictures over to the police and you can send me back to jail for bribery. We are equal. It's a good trade, Paddy Pape."

The statement had a great impact on Paddy. This Indian wasn't some con trying to shake him down. This was a man demanding his dignity, risking incarceration in the process. Paddy inhaled from the joint passed back to him, sniffled, then said, "Everybody needs friends."

"Just do everything by the law," Cobb said. "Just pretend this never happened. I need those forms filed and the reports written. We still have to go through the motions."

"I understand completely," Paddy said.

"We've smoked your smoke and we've agreed on terms," Cobb said.

"We have," Paddy said.

They shook hands and concluded their first meeting. As Cobb was exiting the door, Paddy said, "Oh, but you have to see a therapist. I already sent the forms to the ministry."

Cobb turned. "Are you fucking kidding me?"

Paddy looked up like a helpless puppy. "I assessed you as needing anger management counselling, based on your file." There was a brief silence, after which Paddy said, "If you had come on time this wouldn't have happened."

"Ah, fuck," Cobb said.

FAG

WILL SAT ON A concrete block across the street from Mrs. Duncan's rooming house, smoking a cigarette. He liked to talk out loud to himself. He was always interested to hear what he might say. The community gave him the courage to talk out loud. He no longer regarded it as insane. What is insane about talking to yourself? he asked himself. Nothing is insane about talking to yourself, he answered. The definition of sanity is based on community norms.

There was no spring bite left in the air and there probably wouldn't be any bite until mid-October. He lit another cigarette as he butted the first under his foot, inhaling and running a hand through his now shoulder-length dirty blond hair. He hadn't cut it and stopped washing it altogether. He wore the same pants for seven days straight. He changed his underwear three times a week. He bought all his clothes at thrift shops. He shaved once or twice a week.

A fat man, in pants that revealed the crack in his buttocks and with shirt tails blowing up over his protruding belly, stumbled along the street. The man had a thick red mustache, a fat round face, and transplanted red hair. He looked like a banged-up, fiftysomething Cabbage Patch doll. He stooped and scooped a couple of feet away from Will. An enormous and fierce-looking black dog, maybe a cross between a Doberman and a shepherd, circled around him. The man scooped up the shit with a plastic bag over his hand and threw it and the bag into a second plastic bag. He knotted the bag then walked a couple of steps up a small grass hill. He stopped and stood in front of Will, stared at him and said, "Are you a fag?" Then he grinned from ear to ear.

Will closed his eyes. He didn't want to see what was around him anymore. Pity and passion are compassion. It is from the passions that compassion develops. Will opened his eyes quickly. His heart skipped a beat. The voice that answered the last question was not his and he realized he had asked it aloud. He could hardly tell the difference anymore.

EXCHANGE

ROBERT WAS ON THE other side of the garbage Dumpster in the parking lot behind the Dolphin restaurant. Will had left his attic room to have a cigarette. Robert had been cleaning. He was picking up bottles, papers and debris and was throwing it all into the Dumpster. He had made quite a noise, which had wakened Will. It was one of the reasons he had come out to have a cigarette.

Will had walked across the street and when Robert saw him he'd stopped what he was doing and come over for a cigarette, and that was how the conversation started, shortly after midnight in the middle of the week.

"There's nothing quite like that image of Christ, is there, Robert?" Will asked.

"What do you mean?" Robert asked.

They were sitting down on adjacent sides of the Dumpster, their backs against it.

"Well, the image, you know the crucifix. They're all over the house I'm living in. I have to think about the crucifix. I was raised a Catholic. It can't be escaped, Robert. There's something inescapable about a thing that was in your bedroom from the very beginning of your life. There is a man dying in your eyesight every day, the last thing you see before you go to sleep every night. I didn't see a crucifix for four years at school, Robert, four years, and now I have to see them again every day."

Will threw his half-smoked cigarette away. It tasted horrible. He sat silent for a moment.

"It's one of the great images of all time. I think the Bible might be the first tabloid story in history. For sure. The first. The first tabloid story is a homicide."

"Agreed, and that would account for the phenomenal success of the Bible. It's got murder, sex, celebrity. I don't think there's a better selling book in the world. The mystery of it sells. Who killed Jesus? We know what killed Jesus, Robert. Market forces killed Jesus. It makes you think about economics. It's all economics, Robert. I'm just starting to get a handle on what I studied for four years, and I graduated at the top of my class. Jesus was a bad economist. He had no interest in building a home on earth. It's almost like he had contempt for the world. I mean, what was the deal in the temple? He chased out the money lenders. How can you reach out to the merchant class if you have no respect for property? That whole temple thing, you know, with the money lenders, that was a little radical. An economist shouldn't over-participate in a society, although some monetary and fiscal theorists might disagree. That's why they killed Socrates, too. I don't buy that corrupting-the-youth crap for a minute. He disrupted the economy. For people to live together they have to have an exchange of some sort, you know, some sort of meaningful exchange, and that's how we define a community, an exchange. People need to give and they need to get. That's how we all feel as though we're in a community, Robert."

"Give and get," Robert said from the other side of the Dumpster.

"Right. We give and we get. What Jesus was suggesting — and here's where it gets crazy, Robert — Jesus was suggesting an exchange without any commodities besides compassion. Now, compassion, to my understanding, Robert, is a highly unstable balance of passions. That's not my theory entirely. How can compassion be a commodity? There's no way to measure it. Volume is a measure whether maximizing an economy or not. The weird thing about it is that the modern message of Christ, the crucifix itself, is the template for the modern world. It doesn't get any simpler than that, a crucifix. Anywhere you go in the world, if you see that cross, you know it's a franchise on the Bible. You know the whole story. It's the most effective logo in the history of marketing. Any corporation that franchises is competing with the crucifix. It's in more places than McDonald's."

A bright light appeared and then another. They were the headlights of a car. Then there was a third light, a searchlight. It was a police cruiser. A door opened and closed. Will heard footsteps.

"Stand up please," a voice said.

Will stood.

"Do you have any identification?"

"No."

"Where do you live?"

"There," Will said, pointing to his house across the street.

"What are you doing out here?"

"Nothing."

"We got a call that there were bottles smashing and someone shouting."

"Oh, that was me talking."

"Talking? Who are you talking to?"

"Robert."

"Robert?"

"My friend. He's on the other side of the Dumpster."

Private Constable Richard Chase went around the Dumpster with his flashlight. When he returned he said, "Nobody there, kid."

"He was just there a second ago."

"Name?"

"William Tobe."

"How old are you, William?"

"Twenty."

"Hearing any voices tonight, William?"

"No."

"Having any visions tonight, William?"

"Tonight? No. Not tonight."

"Are you living in a home, William?"

"I live in that home across the street, the one I just showed you."

"That's the home they put you in?"

"That's the home I live in."

"Here's what we need to do," Constable Chase said, "you need to walk around for a few minutes, just calm down —"

"I am calm."

"I know that, but just stay out here for a few minutes, then go home and go to bed, because if I get called back here tonight, I'm going to have to take you down to the police station, and you're going to have to stay there until we get a hold of your worker."

"My worker?"

"Your social worker."

"I don't have a worker."

"You don't have a worker?"

"No."

"How long have you been living in the home?"

"Forty-three days."

"Forty-three days?"

"Yes, sir."

"Why forty-three days? Why not six weeks, or a month and a half?"

"I was counting the days because I fasted for the first forty days I was here."

"You didn't eat for forty days?"

"That is correct, sir."

"Why did you do that?"

"Because Jesus did it, sir."

"Jesus?"

"Yes, Jesus."

"I need you to walk around for a few minutes and then go home, William. Do you understand?"

"I do, sir."

"Good then," Chase said. With that he departed.

Will watched the cruiser back out of the parking lot. He watched the headlights disappear around the corner, and then, as if from nowhere, Cobb was standing right beside him.

"What did that fuck want?"

"He told me to stop making noise."

"Fuck him," Cobb said.

"Exactly," Will said, and he turned to look at Cobb. "Have you seen Robert?"

"Nope."

Cobb spat onto the asphalt.

"You fasted for forty days?"

PART TWO

SUMMER

TOTEM

Cobb walked through the lobby of the Gladstone Hotel and saluted Jimmy at the front desk. He bounced down the stairs, stepped into the night, and turned right on Queen Street. The light was red and he stood at the intersection and watched the activity around him. He had on a three-quarter black leather jacket. It was a little heavy for the weather. His choice was that or a sweatshirt. Another truckload of smokes was coming the following day. Cobb was making an extra five thousand dollars a week on top of his salary with the sewer company. He was going for his weekly meeting with his parole officer. Paddy Pape was a victim, just like Cobb, a brother outside the circle around the queen's fire, and a good customer for the smokes.

Cobb watched a police cruiser pull to the side of the road a half block ahead to talk to a couple of streetwalkers. Cops were the worst of the worst. They spoke with the robes who spoke with the spirit of judgment, but the cops never understood what the robes said, they never felt the comfort of the spirit of judgment. They never felt protected. It made them fearful and angry in their hearts.

Cobb watched Sheila, his neighbour down the hall at the Gladstone, walk away from her friend and turn into an alley. The cop talked to the other girl through the window of his cruiser. Cobb walked past. He stopped a half block ahead and turned around when he was in a thick group of people at a streetcar stop. The cop talked another two or three minutes then pulled away, past Cobb in the middle of the streetcar group. Cobb doubled back and turned into the alley just before the alley Sheila had gone into. He jogged to the back end and hid behind a garbage Dumpster.

It took one minute for the cruiser to appear on the back lane. The cop had circled the block and returned to make his rendezvous with Sheila. Cobb ducked as the headlights fell on the Dumpster.

Cobb moved from behind the bin. The cop had parked only a couple of metres into the alley. It was pitch black behind the cruiser. There were no lights in the alley. The cruiser was turned off. The side door opened and the interior light popped on for a second. Sheila slid into the cruiser and closed the door. Cobb saw a soft glow inside the car. It disappeared almost immediately. He saw a softer light, almost imperceptible, as soft as the end of some burning substance, like tobacco. He could hear the murmur of voices. They were speaking comfortably with each other. The soft glow returned and then disappeared again. He could see the silhouettes of their heads and the shoulders of the cop. Sheila's silhouette disappeared. Cobb observed the interior of the vehicle. There was only one silhouette. Cobb stood with his back against the wall of the alley and waited. Five minutes later the passenger door opened and closed. He heard Sheila's heels on the asphalt. She was coming out the back way toward Cobb. He saw her and crouched. There was a pile of empty boxes that smelled of rotting produce. They hid Cobb well. When she was a pace past Cobb's position he stood up behind her, grabbed her around the chest, squeezed, and put one of his giant hands over her mouth.

"Tap my leg once for weed, twice for crack, what did you smoke with the cop? Do you understand?"

She nodded her head then tapped his leg once.

"Is he stoned? Once for yes, twice for no."

She tapped his leg once.

"I'm going to let you go. If you turn around and look at me I'll do you and the cop, do you understand?"

She tapped his leg once. He let her go and she walked down the back lane without looking back. She didn't walk fast. She just walked out.

Cobb picked up a rock and walked to the driver side of the cruiser. The light was on inside and the young constable was writing in his notebook. The interior light blinded him to anything outside the car. Cobb was silent. The young constable didn't know there was a giant Indian standing on the other side of his window. Cobb smashed the glass with the stone. He noted the look of terror on the cop's face, then rendered him unconscious with a single blow to the chin, certain that it all happened so quickly the cop wouldn't be able to tell the detectives whether his assailant was black, yellow, seven or four feet tall. Cobb took the man's badge and all the bullets from his gun. He left the gun because he didn't want it. He didn't need it. They would triple the manpower to find the culprit if a gun was taken. The city would loosen purse strings, bend the law, do what it had to do to find a person who took a cop's gun. A gun was a cop's totem. Their spirit of judgment lived within their guns. They would look for a cop's gun the way they looked for a missing child.

LOTTERY

COBB BELIEVED THAT NOTHING summed up better the white man's ridiculous obsession with his own existence than life insurance. Nothing so belittled the majesty of the human spirit as life insurance. In its web of complexity the queen's economy suggested a need for this kind of insurance. If the Creator wants to take you out the insurance companies can limit the financial difficulties experienced by your loved ones with a policy. They'll hardly know you're gone, except for the fact that you will be gone. Keep the machine going. God cares for he who cares for himself. The insurance companies were second only to the banks.

Cobb could see death. It was one of the dark gifts given to him by Crow. But he could not predict death. There was still chance to contend with, and there were still other forces that diluted death. There was no lust in death. There was patience, but, when a person was close to death in themselves, its presence could be apprehended, and life insurance policies were a lottery Cobb knew how to win.

He filled out a few policies. They were expensive to maintain and the people he was insuring smoked, drank and had used drugs, all of which he openly declared on the forms. The premiums were much higher and the insured had to go for a physical, but when death was around a person it could be as little as six months to call them out of the world. Death never stopped whispering once it found someone to whisper into.

There was a knock at Cobb's door. He got off the bed and opened it. Martin Fisher walked in and sat down at the table. He took out some tobacco and started to roll himself a cigarette. His hands shook and his hair was dry and wild and springing off his head like wild grass. Martin was forty-four years old, but he looked closer to sixty. He had been on the streets since he was sixteen. Cobb felt a deep movement inside of him as he shut the door and looked at Marty shaking his way to a tightly rolled cigarette. Cobb walked over and handed him a Marlboro.

"Thanks," Marty said.

Cobb sat down and got right to business.

"Occupation?"

"Jesus, Cobb."

"Right, sorry. You play the harmonica, don't you?"

"I do." And with that joyous admission, Marty pulled a harmonica out of his pocket and began to play a little tune.

"Nice," Cobb said, and he wrote *musician* in the occupation field of the form.

"Address?"

"Here."

"Right."

Cobb wrote his parole officer's address down. Paddy Pape used a communal mailbox and Cobb had already had the key duplicated. When he was finished the form and Marty had signed it, he handed him a carton of cigarettes.

"Geez, thanks, Cobb."

OXYGEN

DOROTHY LEANED ON THE counter at the Dolphin. She walked over to Cobb and Will with the coffee pot. "More coffee?"

Cobb shook his head and blew her a kiss.

"I'll have a refill," Will said.

She refilled his coffee cup and walked back over to the waitress stand.

Will continued.

"If the market is going to sustain itself, then the market is going to have to redefine wealth. Money won't go another hundred years. It's an expired commodity. The market is no different than an individual. We think about dreams when there's wood in the furnace and food in our stomachs.

"If the market is going to sustain itself for another hundred years, artificial wealth must be translated back to real wealth. I'm not talking about the gold standard here. If this keeps going the way it's going, within twenty years oxygen will be a commodity. You don't actually sell oxygen. You sell by cubic tonne of carbon monoxide reduction. It works on bonds determined by accredited botanists. The way I see it, pretty soon you're going to see chartered and bonded botanists with legal power in the world and by legal power I mean the power to set a wealth standard on land, based on oxygen production. They'll go at the formulas on this like medieval alche-mists. How many trees per square foot, what kind of oxygen production, essentially every factor that would go into the measurement of oxygen. Then, if the market responds correctly, there will be a thriving market for carbon bonds. People will pay to breathe, because no other transactions are possible without oxygen. Governments will have to pay money to the undeveloped countries to sustain conservation areas, and they'll get that money by taxing citizens. The market itself will have to redefine wealth. If a person were to start buying now, and I don't think it's too expensive, yet, they could probably get land in Nicaragua, real dense and tropical forest, for maybe $50 US per hectare. And I know that some of the governments, like Costa Rica, already give a conservation grant if you don't develop the land. I'm telling you, nature is the next big economy. It's a full circle. The whole economy is going home. Did you know, eco means household, from the Latin *oeco*, and the earth is our home? The market will correct itself, and the story will be whole again. The economy will return to a natural order, kind of like God as the chairman of the US Federal Reserve. Or, if the market doesn't correct itself, then, probably — but I'm not sure — but we'll probably descend into anarchy and chaos, market correction or chaos, one or the other, but, from a reasonable risk position, I mean, given the possible payoff, it is possible to start thinking about an oxygen monopoly, or a significant minority position in the market."

Cobb folded back his paper and looked at Will.

"You're not from around here, are you?"

"No, I came here because I had a vision."

"A vision?"

"Yes."

"What are you doing now?"
"Nothing."
"You want a job?"
"All right."

CREATION STORY

MS. GOLDMAN MADE A note with her Montblanc pen in her leather bound notebook. Persey watched her hand move. It was a graceful movement: unrushed, attentive to the flow of the written language, conscious of it in a way that showed respect, self-awareness and intimacy. Every single thing a person did was a tell. Persey had learned this years ago, learned it from her mother, learned that all behaviour is laced with an undercurrent of consciousness that spoke volumes about the person's interior. Ms. Goldman was a together person. Her handwriting told Persey that this was her time and her space and that she was completely in control of it. Sometimes Persey wondered what Ms. Goldman was like outside of the office with leather furniture, a restored nineteenth century oak desk that looked prime ministerial in its grandeur, the three Persian rugs (genuine silk and wool) and, of course, the Montblanc pen.

"And so," Ms. Goldman went on, "you feel you are not being validated."

"Yes."

"And how does that make you feel?"

"Non-existent."

"How is your romantic life?"

"Non-existent."

"Do you feel that perhaps your attitude is affecting the feeling that men get from you, maybe telling them to back off and go away?"

"I don't know. What attitude are you referring to?"

"The attitude that you are non-existent."

"Is that an attitude?"

"If you feel it and you hold the feeling inside you as true then it has no option but to express itself as an attitude."

"Yes. I see."

Ms. Goldman waved the magic Montblanc again. Persey had begun to have grave misgivings about psychology. It seemed apparent to her what a sham the whole process was when she was the patient. What was being proffered? That the gangling minutiae that was a person's life was somehow manageable? She felt sure she was in the grip of something far fiercer and far more affecting than an attitude of non-existence.

"I think that is good for today, Persey. Perhaps you would be so kind as to reflect on your self-effacement this week and then be in a position to discuss it next week."

"All right."

Ms. Goldman stood and smiled. They never touched at the end of a session. They never shook hands. They never patted shoulders. It was a strange relationship, therapist and patient, so intimate and yet so cold. Persey stood. They smiled. Ms. Goldman walked her to the door. Persey opened it and departed.

It was five o'clock and the streets were busy. Ms. Goldman's office was in Parkdale. The neighbourhood was not nearly as dilapidated as some sections of US cities, but by Toronto standards it was bottom-shelf. The western perimeter of the city centre — ten to fifteen blocks west of the skyscrapers, the bank buildings, the investment houses, Bay Street — consisted mainly of three- and four-storey brick buildings, storefronts, coffee shops, taverns, TV repair shop. The apartments above these were cockroach-infested, under-maintained dwellings owned by the sub-literate thugs who circumvented the Landlord and Tenant Act and took a good portion of their tenants' welfare cheques from them. The locals were a combination of delusionals, bail recognizance breachers and other voluntary and involuntary seekers of anonymity. Persey liked the community. It provided a release by proxy, the close association to her inner state.

There had always been a building that had a great appeal for her, the Gladstone Hotel, right at the corner of Queen Street and Dufferin Street, but she had never had the courage to enter it before. On the ground floor was a tavern that was as precise in the definition of tavern as an establishment could be. It could have been transported to eighteenth century London and not been out-of-place. The bar was long and wooden. The tables were round and wooden, and had four seats around each. The tavern was always occupied but never full.

Persey walked through the front lobby of the Gladstone Hotel. Two garishly dressed women quarrelled with the older man at the front desk about their bill. From what she overheard, Persey deduced they were two monthly habitants who claimed, to the rejection of the front desk person, that they had paid a security deposit when they moved in. Without allowing herself to feel guilt for judgment, Persey concluded the women were prostitutes. She walked past the commotion at the front desk, turned right into a small hallway, and entered the tavern. Hardly a head turned to look at her. She mulled over whether or not to take a table or to make the more daring move of sitting at the bar. She chose the bar, as daring was the motif for her day.

Persey sat down beside a man near the middle of the bar. He was large and his back was to her, as he was engaging another patron to his right. His long black braid reached his waist. The bartender walked over and asked her what she would have.

"Molson Canadian draft," she said.

The man to her right glanced part way in her direction as if to absorb her presence into his understanding without actually looking at her. She caught half his large face and one almond eye before he turned back to his occupation, negotiations with the man in black leather to his right. Her beer came at the same time the man in black leather shook the large man's hand and left the bar, at which time the large man turned to her and said nothing. She held his eyes for a short moment then looked into her beer. She was aware that he kept staring at her. She pretended not to notice but began to think that her daring motif was an overestimation of her abilities. She didn't belong in there with her fancy shoes and pant suit.

"Smokes?"

"Excuse me?" she asked, looking at the large man and noticing for the first time that he was not Caucasian.

"You want to buy smokes?"

"I don't smoke."

"Make you look sexy."

She blushed.

"You like to look sexy. No reason for shoes and clothes like that unless you want to look sexy."

She looked herself over from feet to chest.

"Nothing wrong with looking sexy."

"No, I guess not," she said.

"Charlie," the large man said. "Another beer for me and the sexy lady."

"Oh, no, not me, I have to go."

"Go where?"

"Home."

"Where's home?"

"West of here."

"Mississauga?"

"No."

"That's an *Indian* word, you know."

"I did know that."

"I believe you."

"Are you Indian?"

"Mohawk. Otherwise I owe a lot of sales tax."

She laughed.

Charlie brought two beers and placed one in front of each of them.

"All right," she said. "One more."

"Makes you look sexy, drinking beer in here."

"Do I not look sexy anyway?"

"Yes, but more sexy is always better. You've never been in here before, have you?"

"No."

"Why not?"

"I don't know. You come here a lot?"

"Yes."

"You live in Parkdale?"

"Yes."

"I work in Parkdale at the mental health centre."

"Doctor?"

"Studying to be one."

"Medicine woman you are."

"What's that?"

"That's someone who heals the hidden body, the body that walks the invisible plains."

"That's beautiful."

"That's Mohawk."

"It must be very ... it must be a very good feeling to know who you are ... to be able to go back to stories that form a line of existence since the beginning of the earth."

"You getting heavy on me now, Doc?"

"Persey. My name is Persey."

"Cobb," he said, and he extended his hand in greeting.

She reached back in response and her hand disappeared inside his. It was as big as half her head.

"All those stories. All those answers. More and more I am coming to the conclusion that we're all just kids on the inside, little kids, and the stories we hear that make us believe there is an answer to everything, like these stories from your people, they let us be what we are."

"Except the white man has no more story. His dream is a beaten enemy, a forced labourer, a slave," Cobb added.

They sat and they drank in silence for a moment.

"What do you do?"

"Sewer maintenance."

"You like that?"

"That's what they gave me."

"They?"

"Work program."

"Are you...."

"A convicted felon?"

"Yes."

"Yeah. But don't worry. It wasn't anything violent. It was a white man's crime, only I'm red so they put me away."

"Embezzlement?"

"Tax evasion, but I still went to the penitentiary."

"I thought you were exempt from taxes?"

"Me too."

"There must be more to it than that."

"Always is."

"So...."

"Cigarettes. Taxes. Government says I defrauded them. I never joined their government."

"You have to remit business sales tax to the government. It's only fair. It's the government."

Cobb turned to face her by spinning on his bar stool. "So, you want to get a room?" he asked.

"What?"

"A room upstairs."

"What for?"

"Sex."

"You're asking me to have sex?"

"What would you choose between feeling and suffering?"

"Suffering."

"Why?"

"I don't know."

"Maybe because it's the power of the dream ... our lives ... to keep it all going, to keep it in motion, to have a clear knowing that we're alive."

"That's a strong idea."

"People like us have to find feeling where it finds us. There's no need for people like us to be penitent. It builds prisons of our spirits."

"Okay," she said, "okay, I'll get a room."

UNDERGROUND

It was a shitty job but somebody had to do it, and why not somebody just out of prison. There were plenty of people to do these jobs in Toronto, plenty of the hungry and the needy and the desperate. Cobb could not have been assigned a more humiliating job. If he was not actually digging with a shovel or aiding a backhoe with a dig, he was in a tunnel, trying to find a blockage or some other thing for which the paroled Indian was sent into the shit. He had to do it. Failure to report for a job on parole was not something that Paddy could fix. There is give and take in any functioning relationship.

The refuse of a city was mind-boggling. The little light on his hardhat illuminated truth down there. Man is defined more accurately by what he doesn't want to look at than by what he wants to look at. Sure, it didn't make sense for anyone to want to look at their own shit, to smell it, to step in it. There was logic to the decision to send all the shit under the city, off to the recycling plant to be cleansed with powerful chemicals and then released back into Lake Ontario.

The white man was ashamed of what he was. He was ashamed of being human, ashamed of being an animal, ashamed of being loved by the Creator. The trickster gives and the trickster takes. Cobb only had to see what the trickster was trying to show him there in the tunnels. Cobb only had to see the weakness in their system, all the wires, the communication lines, the power lines. The white man was naked in his tunnels. He was exposed. Cobb had already paid someone at City Hall to get the plans for the sewer system, and he was studying them at home. He could make his away around most of the city through the tunnels. There were rats, snakes and other things that might deter a less determined man than Cobb, but the trickster had taught him that obstacles were hidden opportunities.

THERAPY

COBB HAD BEEN SITTING in the waiting room of Dr. Bluette's office for ten minutes or so. It was long enough to make him uncomfortable. He fidgeted with his hands. He tugged at the bunched cotton underwear pinching into his groin. He looked out the window. He looked at the wall hangings, a few prints.

Twice a month for an hour Paddy had set up for him to see the therapist. She was not the usual Canada Corrections employee filling a day for a guaranteed pay stub. She only saw a few convicts on parole. It was a small part of her practice. "Giving back," she called it. She was a professional acquaintance of Paddy Pape's. She spoke highly of him, a man she described as dedicated to the betterment of the marginalized. Cobb loved that word, marginalized. It was laced with the guilt of semi-aware white people, and it had helped him out numerous times in court through his adolescence. "Your honour," the legal-aid lawyer would say. "My client is part of a marginalized people." At sentencing hearings, "Your Honour, we would petition the court that Mr. Seymour be given a sentence that reflects his marginalized status." Dr. Bluette bought in heavily to this concept. Why wouldn't she? She made a whack of dough for doing next to nothing, and she did it on the backs of the marginalized. It amazed Cobb how white people could be so smart and so stupid at the same time. Dr. Bluette had no sense of the world behind the world. She thought dreams were the key to the psyche. She didn't believe in a spirit like Cobb's that could walk the invisible plains and be given a mission by Crow.

Cobb was merciful with her. He didn't make any trouble. His only condition with Paddy was that the sessions be on work time, not evening time, so he could actually look forward to them. A 2 p.m. session could get him out of the sewers for a whole afternoon. Cobb did no preliminary work on Dr. Bluette. She didn't have any real power over him, but he did take advantage of the access to information her office provided him. Dr. Bluette kept all her files in cabinets. She had drawers full of tape-recorded sessions with patients, going back as far as ten years. It was the perfect place for Cobb to get more information on the white man, further his unofficial research into the worst creature the Creator had ever made. There was no security whatsoever beyond a locked door. It was tougher to break into Paddy's place. At least he had the dog, King.

The Toronto Police Force had its own psychiatrist, but Richard Chase had wanted to go outside the force. There was a strange way in which things said in confidence where the blue-shield society existed made their way into the ears of that body blue in its totality — cops gossiped. They could be terribly cruel. The week after Chase got out of the hospital there was a pair of panties and a Kotex pad taped to his locker when he got back. Some shit heel on the street had stolen his badge, was showing it to his friends, flashing it about town, maybe using it to fake being a cop himself? It was a horror story. There were the other things too, the pins in his jaw, the headaches, the bad dreams and the fear.

The fear was the worst thing of all. In his first year on the force there was a cop who had been jumped and beaten; the fear had gotten into him. Chase's brothers and sisters in blue compared it to a high steelworker who lost his nerve. There were men, according to these urban stories, who could work high steel all their lives, from eighteen onward, then, one day, with no warning, they lost their nerve. They found themselves out on a ledge, unable to move, frozen, suddenly intimately aware of how high up they were, of what a fall from that height would do to them — a closed casket, teeth scattered for a block, gold fillings washed into a sewer in the next big rain — and they just stood there, dumbfounded. They didn't cry for help. They didn't ask someone to come over. When the work they were doing was left undone, and it became obvious to everyone that there was a stoppage, the crane operator found himself hanging a load with nobody coming over to unhook it, then they would start looking for the problem. They would find the man paralyzed on a beam of steel in the middle of the sky. It was the Mohawks who found them. They never lost their nerve. They were the best high steelworkers in the world. Nature had given them an unassailable confidence in the sky, bolstering the myth of an eagle as spirit guide, guardian of the sky. But Chase had frozen. He had not returned to the street since he got knocked out, since his jaw was broken, his badge was stolen, his dignity snuffed like a candle on a canoe. He was on a disability pension.

Chase wasn't much for the sentimental, the consciously sensitive, the overtly empathetic. He had seen the worst scum in society on a day-to-day basis. He arrived at apartments where husbands had knocked out wives, wives had stabbed husbands, children had been beaten and dogs had been poisoned.

Dr. Bluette had written extensive case notes: *Patient attacked at night while on duty, broken jaw, pins in jaw. Police badge stolen. Bullets from gun stolen. Patient experiencing difficulties re-entering the workforce.*

The door opened and a sophisticated woman in slacks and blouse smiled warmly at Cobb. She had salt-and-pepper hair cut shoulder length. The grey in her hair made her look important. She could have coloured it out, but that would have been vain. She preferred the grey. She gestured for Cobb to come forward. He went into the office and took his usual seat. Dr. Bluette sat behind her desk.

"So, Randall, how are you feeling today?" she asked.

COURIER

WILLIAM TOBE'S LIFE CHANGED when he started working for Cobb. It wasn't a regular job. It was more like self-employment. He could make his own hours and the deadlines he lived by were not thirty minute lunches and fifteen minute breaks. His was a physically demanding job. He had to walk to the garage in Parkdale where Cobb stored the cigarettes, load the pickup truck, drive through the city and make deliveries through back doors of taverns, convenience stores, bingo halls and other establishments. He had to collect the money. This was not always an easy task. He was a "little soft with collections," as Cobb put it, but the money always showed up sooner or later and nobody ripped him off.

The suppliers had their own keys to the garage. Will never met them. Every few days there was new inventory. Cobb left a cellphone in the garage for Will. Every morning Will checked the messages on the cellphone. Cobb told him not to take the cellphone home in the evenings or the calls would drive him crazy. In the three weeks Will had been a cigarette runner the record for phone messages in a single day was forty-two; that day he didn't finish his run until just before midnight.

Besides delivering cigarettes, Will was responsible for new business development. He wasn't as brazen as Cobb. He found it difficult to walk into a business and say, "You guys need smokes?" but he did manage to find new clients every week. The business kept expanding. The money was outrageous. Will turned all the cash — and there was nothing but cash in their business — over to Cobb. He asked Cobb if he wanted him to make the bank deposits but Cobb told him he had no bank account. Will could hardly believe it. There was no way Cobb was spending all the money unless he was supporting a small reserve, so Will imagined a big pile of bank notes under Cobb's bed, just like the Japanese had done before the devaluation of the yen. Will realized that Cobb was an economist, albeit a principled economist, which was the worst kind.

Cobb had explained that there was no way to move that kind of money into a bank on a weekly basis and not raise the attention of the bank manager. Cobb explained that bank managers were agents of the queen, under contract with the Canada Revenue Agency, and that they had to report transactions as small as $2,000.

Will explained the concept of incorporation. The business would require a cash-only system, like a restaurant or corner store. Cobb found the ideas risky but attractive. They could have the ATM cards for the corporate account. Will could do the accounting. All they needed was a front man, someone in the system with a social insurance number. Cobb was greatly impressed with Will's knowledge of the world of money. He finally accepted Will's counsel.

On the day of incorporation it was raining. It was always unpleasant to distribute cigarettes when it was raining. Will got wet and the cigarettes got a little wet. It took more time to do a run because drivers on the downtown streets were slower. The rain just dampened everything. The only good thing about that day was that it was short. There had been only twelve messages on the machine that morning. Will finished the day's cigarette run before 11 a.m. This left time for a trip to the Ministry of Consumer and Corporate Affairs. Today was the day.

Will picked up Robert Polski at the Dolphin. He had been there all morning. Will had given him enough money to make sure Dorothy didn't kick him out. They went over the drill twice on the way to the ministry offices. If asked about the nature of the corporation's activities, Robert was to say "no restrictions." A name search was not required. A numbered company was fine. The initial share issuance was two hundred. They were all common shares. Robert wore a suit that Will had bought at Goodwill, and Will had fitted him with an adult diaper.

Will pulled up in front of the ministry and Robert got out. Will watched him climb the stairs and disappear through the revolving door. He felt like a proud parent.

GUARDIAN

WILL PICKED UP ROBERT Polski's thrift-shop suit from the dry cleaner's and walked down Queen Street West on that late summer morning, the suit held aloft in its plastic wrap. Will's hair was now cut short and he was clean-shaven. He wore a dark pinstriped suit, a conservative, money suit. He wore a crisp white shirt and a crimson silk tie. This was just another business day for him. Polski, too.

Will opened the door at the Dolphin and the wind chimes sounded. He said hello to Dorothy, and he said hello to Fred, the owner, who was busy cleaning the grill, his cooking whites stained from the breakfast rush.

Will had spent a lot of money in the Dolphin, despite being a non-drinker, and Fred had taken to greeting him as a valued customer, a regular. Dorothy was now more tolerant of Robert. Fred had probably had a talk with her; Polski brought money to the Dolphin. Cobb and Will made sure of this. They also made sure he was well taken care of, what with his suit, tobacco, pocket money. Polski was their CEO. They were 1109897 Ontario Inc.

Will passed the suit to Robert, who took it to the bathroom. Will slid into the booth and Dorothy came over. Will ordered a coffee and a fried egg sandwich on dry whole wheat toast. He was eating again. Robert came out in his suit at the same time Will's sandwich arrived at their table. Will ate quickly, paid, said goodbye to Dorothy, then he and Polski left for the Royal Bank.

The nearest branch of the Royal Bank, the former Merchants Bank of Halifax, founded in 1864, as Will explained to Robert, was seven blocks from the Dolphin. The bank had been started by a small group of Haligonians, true collectivists who put their money together in order to build up the fishing and lumber industries. The irony of it all, Will told Robert on the way to the bank, was that the fish were almost gone, and so was most of the hardwood, but the Royal Bank was bigger than ever.

Will had plenty of time to go over their story with Robert. It was simple and true. Robert Polski had, by law, a handicap; he had a psychological disorder. He was legally required to follow his prescription. His mind was quarantined behind antipsychotic drugs that reshuffled consciousness. A guardian was not a difficult concept for a bank manager to understand. These kinds of arrangements were common. Will explained to Robert, he was his guardian.

They entered through the main door and walked over to the counter. A young woman with black hair and olive skin smiled and listened to their inquiry. She raised a finger delicately and begged a moment's patience while she went to get the right person. A couple of minutes later, a Mr. Kenny was in front of them with his hand extended in greeting. Robert and Will shook his hand. Mr. Kenny was young, but bald. He had a thick, dark moustache. He had the beady little eyes of a rodent. He, like Will, wore a dark pinstriped suit. He couldn't have been much older than thirty. Mr. Kenny escorted them to the back of the bank and into his office. Mr. Kenny asked what he could do for them. Will explained it to him.

Robert, Will explained, wanted to open a corporate account. The president and chief executive officer was Robert Polski. Robert was a schizophrenic under Will's care by way of the Ministry of Health and Long-Term Care, at the behest of the Ministry of Justice. Robert had come into some money by way of a death in the family and the lawyers for the estate hired him, William Tobe, to invest the funds and manage the assets resulting from the trust. Robert Polski had already incorporated and had his articles of incorporation. It was feared by the estate lawyers that, should Robert govern his affairs without guidance, he might find himself in trouble. The volume of capital to be dispersed to him on a biweekly basis was substantial, the dividend of a large trust. The reporting and accounting of these sums had to be undertaken by a qualified person. Will showed Mr. Kenny the letter of guardianship from the lawyer representing the estate of which Robert was the sole beneficiary. The letterhead was none other than A. E. Campbell, QC. Mr. Polski, as Will explained to Mr. Kenny in the detached tone of one accustomed to managing large sums of money, was quite well off. The lawyers managed the trust. William Tobe was simply to manage the flow of dispersals from the trust.

Mr. Kenny made some elementary sales pitches. The bank had a number of products which could prove beneficial. Anticipating this, and knowing it would further his credibility, Will had structured a monthly cash flow, and he had allowed for the bank's participation. Fifteen percent of the biweekly dispersal was to be invested in a medium-risk fund of the bank's choice. Ten percent was to be invested in indemnified bonds of the bank's choosing. Ten percent was to be invested in the blue chip stocks through the bank's wealth management branch. Ten percent was to be allocated to a currency fund, also of the bank's choosing. The percentages would be reviewed quarterly. The automatic withdrawal forms were drawn up immediately and Robert signed them where Will placed his index finger. The rest of the money would serve to cover the expenses of the beneficiary, Robert Polski, and to facilitate his own investment wishes, which, according to Will, centred on ecology and conservation in Latin America. Mr Kenny smiled and nodded his head a lot.

He left the office once to photocopy the letter of guardianship, Robert's birth certificate, social insurance card, and the articles of incorporation for 1109897 Ontario. In one of the silences, when Will had his head bent to a form he was proofreading, Robert looked at Mr. Kenny and said, "Moses was an economist by my interpretation."

"My goodness, that's a remarkable thought, Mr. Polski, sir."

They finished their business in less than half an hour. They shook hands. Robert and Will left. Will had the account documents and an ATM card for 1109897 Inc.

PART THREE

FALL

JEOPARDY

IN COBB'S ROOM ON the fourth floor of the Gladstone the TV was on loud. Cobb was watching *Jeopardy* and smoking cannabis. He also had a block of incense burning because he had no sweet grass. The smoke was thick and the dim and musty hallway outside his door was perfumed with its scent.

What is a Jain?

What is a pimento?

Who is Benjamin Franklin?

Who is Hamlet?

Where is Ecuador?

By Cobb's tabulation, he would still be on *Jeopardy* after four weeks. His answer ratio was ninety percent correct, five percent partially correct, but ruled invalid by the judges, and five percent wrong and(or) unknown.

Thomas Jefferson had run several successful businesses before he was twenty. Physics was a hobby for Einstein. Cobb maintained the city's sewers and absorbed every bit of information around him. He looked hard at every theory, movement, doctrine or philosophy that acquainted itself, accidentally, providentially or by proselytization, with his existence. All were equal and all were subject to his judgment. If someone believed it, Cobb wanted to know it. Beliefs fascinated Cobb.

Jesus was an extraterrestrial? Okay.

The CIA just gave the barest details of the MK ULTRA project, the real program was run by Mengele and sacrificed human life to test the limits of trauma-based conditioning? Okay.

The Pope before last was executed for attempting an audit of the Vatican bank? Okay.

The White Brotherhood keeps the forces of darkness in check? Okay.

Genghis Khan and the Mongol hordes were one of the lost tribes of Israel, as evidenced by the Jewish roots of many of their customs and rituals? Okay.

The American government had been in contact with alien intelligence for more than five decades now? Okay.

A subspecies within the human realm, having reptilian DNA, capable of shape-shifting into reptiles, secretly controls the world? Okay.

Where is Lisbon?

What is a nematode?

Who is Lord Byron?

What is the Spanish Civil War?

What is Lemuria?

There was a knock at the door. Cobb got up and answered it. It was Sheila, the prostitute from down the hall. She had a problem with some guy who was hunting her head. He felt she owed him some money, or some such story. She was not big on details. For two weeks, in these random visits to Cobb's door, she had been hinting at his becoming some kind of pimp to protect her interests. Her plight inspired a small amount of sympathy in Cobb. He also noticed her sweet little ass, its heart-shaped perfection, her flat stomach and respectable B-cups. She had a whore's face, hard and pretty at the same time, a face that didn't know the difference between talking dirty and talking. Cobb hadn't gone out of his way to solve her problem, and he wasn't thrilled to be seen as a pimp in the hotel. He told her that if a grieved party showed up at her door at three o'clock in the morning and Norm, the old night clerk was on duty, she could wake him and he would attempt a peaceful resolution to the situation. For this noble gesture he was awarded the highest prize in the whore's dowry, a freebie.

"Fucking Jimmy, eh, he fucking fucked me again and didn't pay. That fuck isn't telling them anything. He says my rent is still due. I told him I'm going to tell. I'm not paying a dime. I sucked that fat bastard's cock three times already this week. He doesn't wash. And I have to suck that fat bastard's dick and choke. The fucker won't even wear a condom, so I'm swallowing his jizz. And I owe rent? Fuck that."

"Calm down."

"I am. It's just fucking bullshit and I'm tired of it and I don't want this bullshit anymore. I'm sucking that fat bastard's cock to pay the rent and now that fuck thinks I'm his girlfriend and he's getting it for free?"

"Calm down."

"Okay."

She sat on the bed and Cobb walked over, turning his head for a moment to address the final *Jeopardy* question. He unzipped his pants and Sheila took his cock out. Just as she put it into her mouth, he said, "What is Shangri-La?"

SHARING

PERSEY PICKED WILL UP at eight-thirty in front of the donut shop. They drove downtown and parked the car. They got out and walked together, talking about things from Ottawa and things going on in their lives in Toronto. Because he wanted to, and because he needed to, he told her more about the vision he'd had in his dormitory at the University of Ottawa. She had been there as well, on the campus, in the last year of her undergraduate degree, recovering from her suicide attempt, which her mother did not find out about until she graduated and returned to Toronto.

Persey listened politely, because she had been taught to. She said little — this was not a professional relationship. It was a friendship and perhaps an erotic curiosity. She didn't quite know what to make of it. Will didn't seem delusional to her. He briefly mentioned his vision; he spoke almost entirely about economics and public policy. She had met this kind of boy before. He was a typical Ottawa boy. He wasn't insane. He was just a little off. She imagined him in the small attic room he had told her about, surrounded by stacks of books he had been meaning to read. She envied the freedom of his life.

As they walked in the late summer night air, Persey felt a need to share something of herself. After all, that's what distinguishes a personal relationship from a professional one. She wanted to share. She needed to talk. She needed another human being to listen to her. Will seemed perfect. She told him about her life, about the dark forces that took over her mind, the blinding pessimism that occupied her days, the absolute horror of the human condition, the frailty of the mind, the tenuous hold any of them had on reality. She told him in detail about the last attempt she had made at taking her own life. She had thought about it for three weeks. It was her last thought before falling asleep and her first thought upon waking. She finally decided on a straight razor to her wrists. She planned every detail. She secured sedatives to dull the pain. She bought a nice bottle of red wine. She put on a CD of Ivo Pogorelich playing Chopin's Piano Sonata no. 2 in B-flat Minor. She took the sedatives, drew herself a bath, cut her wrists twenty minutes later, poured a glass of wine, took a sip and watched the bath water turn red. She had awakened in the ER. Her roommate had come back early from a visit to Montreal.

Will listened attentively. He told her about noticing her scars at the coffee shop and he how he had been thinking about those scars for two days, how sad they made him, because, after talking to her for five minutes in the coffee shop, he was forced to imagine a world without her and couldn't. He told her he realized that her reality was bigger than his imagination, since he could not imagine her death.

After walking in silence for a while, Will said, "We live in a time when it is dangerous to experience things that can't be shared with others. It leaves us vulnerable to their fears and their reprisals."

Persey was deeply moved by the statement. She asked, "Do you want to get a hotel room?"

He said, "No. No, I can't do that."

INDIAN SUMMER

PADDY APE DIDN'T KNOW that Cobb and Will had gone into business together. He didn't know about Robert Polski. He didn't know that they had incorporated. He didn't know that they were running an investment portfolio at the local Royal Bank into which they had deposited over $240,000. They had sold whole truckloads to single buyers. Cobb could sell a truckload of cigarettes with a phone call. It was remarkable. He had the touch, that magic that makes the capital system work. He could move goods for money and he had an intuitive sense for the threshold, that point where risk is perfectly managed. Cobb knew the channels and currents of all the waters by which he and Will traded. He had preserved the core business in west Toronto. Will still made those deliveries. They would have liked to have served the whole city within the west Toronto model, but it would mean a dozen delivery people, a dozen trucks, group vehicle insurance, a whole truckload of hassles.

The hallway of Paddy's apartment was wet. It was wet every time Will went down there, and the crappy fluorescent light barely lit the place. At the end of the hallway Will knocked on Paddy's door. The door opened and Paddy stood there in his pink housecoat.

Will recognized him immediately, and wondered if Paddy did him. Paddy stared at him a minute, longer than necessary to get a fix on Will.

"I'm Will. I think I've seen you around. We're neighbours. I just came by to see if I could get you to tell Cobb I need cigarettes," Will said.

"I'm Paddy. Randall's here now," Paddy said. He took a longer look at Will. "I love this new Bay Street look on you," he said and then he stood back to allow Will into the apartment. "Jesus, Randall, it's bad enough that I'm not really supervising your parole, now you're selling cigarettes to my neighbours out of my apartment?"

"I didn't tell him to come here," Cobb said.

"No harm, no foul," Paddy responded.

Will sat down. Paddy grabbed a tape off of the shelf, *Pee-wee's Playhouse*, and put it in the VCR. He had the whole series on videotape.

"Can I have another beer?" Cobb asked.

"Get it yourself," Paddy replied.

Paddy sat on a kitchen chair. The legs bent and the frame creaked.

Cobb found a beer in the apartment-sized refrigerator. When he sat again, he winked at Will.

"Randall is looking for a place to stay," Paddy said.

"Where are you staying now?" Will asked.

"I have a room at the Gladstone."

"He's looking for something a little more homey," Paddy said.

"Well, there is a room at my place right now," Will said. "But there's a reason it's still empty. The old lady is very particular."

"Yeah. That's what Paddy was telling me," Cobb said.

"The rent is reasonable but you can't smoke in the house, and the landlady is fussy about a lot of things."

"No problem," Cobb said. "I'm used to living with rules."

"I'll talk to her," Will said. He leaned back and lit a cigarette.

"Listen," Paddy said. "I'm not going to lie to you, Will. Randall is a paroled felon, but I give you my word, he's fully on the path to rehabilitation, and I'm sure he'll have no problem living by Mrs. Duncan's rules."

There was a pause and nobody looked at anybody, and then Paddy added, "I just thought it was fair to tell you that, Will. I didn't mean to embarrass you, Randall."

"I know, Paddy. It's okay."

"You see, Will, he's as gentle as a lamb."

"Where were you tonight?" Cobb asked Will.

"Out with a girl I knew in Ottawa."

"You have a girlfriend now?" Paddy asked.

"She's not my girlfriend."

"Oh, Jeeeesus, doesn't anybody get to suck that cock of yours?" Paddy asked.

BLOOD OF THE MONTH

THREE WEEKS HAD PASSED since Will and Persey had gone out. They hadn't phoned each other regularly. Persey was in a foul mood when she met up with Will. Her thoughts were dark. Will was worried about her. He didn't want her to try to kill herself again. Nothing good could come of that. How would he feel if someone he had met and shared a bit of life with died? Persey was going on and on about menstruation.

There is a time of the month that women bleed, she told him. Men remember this only when they begin to see the signs of stress and the pain of the blood, or, more notably, when there is no blood. The blood of the month is a life ritual for the fertile woman. Persey's mother had coined the phrase "blood of the month." She had studied menstruation in other cultures, most notably Native-Canadian culture. Native women were known to paint with their menstrual blood. She was an expert in pre-menstrual stress. She gave lectures and seminars around the globe on the blood of the month. Persey had been raised to take that time, pain and stress, and turn it all over to her creative power, the God within her. It was her mother's contention that the blood of the month must be a time of great creativity and insight because the relationship between growth and pain was central to her interpretation of her faith, her Presbyterian heritage. "Why would God give pain without reward?" she asked rhetorically in many of these seminars and lectures. "Why would heaven ask us to bear this burden, unless there was some payback, some insight, some closer relationship to creation?" The saviour had bled on the cross and, true, he'd had his moment of doubt and weakness, but it had only made him stronger. A woman died a small death in the blood of the month. That is what it all came down to. This small death was opportunity for a small resurrection.

"Is your mother a lesbian?" Will asked.

"No. Mother is a celibate," Persey said.

Will found it very odd that a sixty-year celibate psychiatrist had dedicated her life to the female reproductive process, as shaped by religion and New Age philosophy. Persey agreed and confessed that she found the more eccentric of her mother's ramblings a little cultic, but this was not her concern today. Her concern was that she had not received the blood of the month. The tab on the home pregnancy test was blue. She was pregnant. There would be no small resurrection in a few days. There would be creation in eight months.

"Who is the father?" Will asked.

"That's irrelevant," Persey answered. "I didn't need a father and this child doesn't need one."

Persey's mind had already calculated what she would do if she were to ever get pregnant again. She would have the child. She would kill no more. There was no great moral reasoning in her decision. It was just that after two abortions already, she felt she had used up her publicly funded allotment. They were like emergency flares. She had fired two and to fire a third would be an abuse. The other two were genuine. At the age of fifteen, she had become impregnated by her neighbour. She was able to maneuver the evacuation of that fetus with little difficulty, though she had to lie a little to keep her mother out of it. The second pregnancy was the result of an affair with her teaching assistant in a second-year anthropology course.

"Eugene Feldman?" Will said.

"Oh," Persey said, "you took that course?"

"Geez, was that even legal?" Will asked. "How old were you in second year?"

"I was seventeen when Eugene and I were lovers. I never told him about the pregnancy."

Will sipped his coffee. An uneasy feeling in his gut grew, as he contemplated Persey's situation.

"When are you going to tell your mother?" he asked her.

Persey shrugged her shoulders.

This was Persey's third pregnancy. She had an almost Catholic fertility. She wondered aloud if she had been born in one of those crappy Catholic places of the world — like the Azores or Mexico — if she might be one of those women who had twelve or more children, a baby factory for the pope, a one woman response to the dwindling birth rate of the first world, and in particular, the white race. Pope John Paul the Second was the antithesis of the modern age. Her mother sometimes said he made being Christian an embarrassment. Should she tell her mother about this pregnancy? What good would it do? Persey's suicide attempt had been almost too much for her mother. Why burden her with this pregnancy? Persey thought there was a strange symmetry to her current situation. "Mother, I'm going to have a baby," not "Mother, I want to die."

ROOMMATE

SUNDAY WAS THE BEST day to approach Mrs. Duncan. She was always cordial on Sundays, no matter what transpired during the week. Mrs. Duncan's opinion of Will, which declined from week to week, had put him further from the pleasant graces of her company, her tea and her parlour.

He knocked lightly on her door.

"Yes?" Slight and tenuous, Mrs. Duncan's voice sounded from the depths of her parlour.

"It's me, Will, Mrs. Duncan."

The door opened slowly and Mrs. Duncan emerged in a bright print dress. Her long red hair had been let down.

"Yes, Mr. Tobe?"

He smiled and held the smile for several seconds, which seemed like an eternity in the vestibule, in the hope that she might invite him into the more relaxed environment of the parlour. He thought that the more time he had to talk to her, and the more relaxed the circumstances, the better was his chance of dropping his query in the most casual of ways. She made no overture toward tea in the parlour and he realized he was going to have to wing it from the vestibule.

"Hello, Mrs. Duncan. How are you?"

"I'm quite well, Mr. Tobe. Thank you for asking."

"That's nice, anything new?"

"No."

"Same here, Mrs. Duncan. Just one day at a time, I guess."

"Yes."

"Yes, well, it's about the room, Mrs. Duncan."

"Is there anything wrong?"

"Quite the contrary, Mrs. Duncan. Everything is fine, just fine. It's the vacant room I'd like to talk to you about. I was wondering if you were planning on renting it out again?"

"It has crossed my mind, yes, Mr. Tobe. I just have to get around to placing the advertisement. I dislike the process so, the people knocking on the door, the phone calls."

Will smiled and nodded. "Well, that's just why I wanted to talk to you, Mrs. Duncan. I have a friend, a very nice young man. He's new in town and he's looking for a place to stay."

"A friend of yours?"

"Yes. We went to school together."

"I see, he's from Ottawa?"

"Campbellford originally."

"Where is that?"

"East of Toronto, before Kingston. North of the 401. A small town."

"Have your friend come by and see me tomorrow."

"He works awkward hours, Mrs. Duncan. He's entrusted me with the task of finding him a place. He did the same for me in Ottawa."

"What does he do?"

"He's in city planning."

"Does he smoke?"

"No, I don't believe he does."

Will knew that, despite what she thought of him, her options were limited when it came to renting. Her house was in Parkdale.

"All right. If he's a friend of yours, Mr. Tobe, he can take the room."

Will smiled. It was time to leave. Cobb had taught him to leave a sales visit right after a deal had been closed. The longer you hung around the more you risked the customer changing her mind.

Will walked over to Paddy's place. His door was open. He was sitting in the loveseat, smoking a cigarette. The television was off. There was no music. King was sleeping on the floor.

"It's okay for Cobb to move in," Will said through the open door.

Paddy snapped out of his stupor and invited Will in with a gesture, but Will stayed in the door frame.

"You are such a sweetheart," Paddy said. "You spoil me. Cobb is really going to appreciate this. It's important that people like him get to know people like you. It helps them break their patterns. It's simple compassion like this that changes the world, Will, not all the fancy experts and professionals, like me. It's people who make the difference, normal people who don't judge them, who just —"

"All right — Jesus — I get it, Paddy."

"So when can Randall move in?"

"Any time now," Will said.

SHOCK

THE RETURN OF MRS. RABINI to the hospital was a black mark on the record of Zolfax. It wasn't the drug's failings. It was the stubborn insistence of the patient not to use the drug, not even to get the prescription filled. She did not stay in contact with her handlers at the hospital. It was unreasonable for Mrs. Rabini to refuse medication and treatment, Persey said as she unloaded in the donut shop at her semi-regular meeting with Will.

Mrs. Rabini's status in the community had been the occasion for an early morning meeting between Persey, Dr. Singh and a group of specialists at the hospital. Persey had asked to be kept abreast of significant changes involving Mrs. Rabini. She'd wanted her endeavours at the hospital to lengthen to a year. A year was a significant investment. It would look very good for future job applications. But when she and her mother agreed to the one-year framework, they had not conceived of a circumstance in which the patient would be so erratic after a few months of treatment. They thought there would be reports to fill out and a simple procedural conclusion to a voluntary one-year study. Persey now had a full course load with her graduate studies, not to mention she being with child. Mrs. Rabini was never meant to be this much work.

"Why don't you just forget about it?" Will asked.

"How can I do that?" Persey asked.

Will had no answer.

Things had gone from bad to worse. When the administration became aware of a patient, the administration believed itself to have a responsibility not only to the patient, but to society at large. Failure to adhere to her prescribed drug regime had forced an aware administration to call a meeting of all health-care professionals involved in her case for 9 a.m. The new recommended treatment for Mrs. Rabini was electric shock therapy.

"They still do that?" Will asked.

"Oh, yeah," Persey said. "Electric shock therapy is still used."

It sent a shiver down Will's spine.

The administration had recommended shocking the old woman into doing what she had been told to do. There had been a legal representative from the drug company at the meeting. He'd worn a dark suit and had sat back from the board table. The drug company had a stake in the process as well. They had sponsored the trial. Hundreds of millions of dollars went into research and development. The pharmaceutical companies spent almost as much on drug trials as they did on advertising. They monitored them very closely. There was much at stake in the outcomes of the approval process.

The administration had reviewed Persey's notes. Everything was read aloud. It was a close scrutiny of her summer months of diligence with Mrs. Rabini and three other patients whom she had been given to supervise. Words had hung in the air — complacent, docile, unresponsive, agreeable — and these words had the power to direct one of nature's most powerful forces, electricity, through the grey matter of a sixty-four-year-old woman.

Dr. Singh had the nervous habit of playing with the keys to his BMW when he was in meetings with people from the senior hospital administration. His fingers had rolled over the shiny little phallus again and again, but he had been careful not to allow it to become too much of a distraction. He had spoken often about the car to Persey, when he'd first leased it in the summer. He had thought about the 700 series, but the lease payments were prohibitive. A 500 series was completely respectable. It was a solid piece of German engineering.

The lawyer from the drug company had sat off, near a corner of the small boardroom, but his physical exclusion hadn't meant the exclusion of his opinion; when he'd spoken, they listened. His voice was power incarnate. Everything he'd said had layers of meaning, and the meanings were always clear: degree of liability, perception of liability and probable compensation. His had been the most authoritative opinion in the room.

"In most circumstances in life the person writing the cheques has an important say in things. The flow of capital is the flow of opportunity," Will said, trying to participate in Persey's unloading.

Persey gave him an odd look.

Persey had been quiet at the meeting. She was not expected to participate unless she was asked. She was a graduate student, not a doctor. It was an honour and a privilege for her to be in the meeting; an exceptional learning opportunity, her mother had said.

The point that had come up again and again around the table was accountability. The senior administrators had made sure that it was never far from the discussion. The hospital had become aware of Mrs. Rabini and, now that it was aware of her, it had a responsibility to the public. Mrs. Rabini could, without benefit of proper medication and therapy, attack another person. If the victim came into the knowledge that Mrs. Rabini had been released with the administration's awareness that she was refusing to take her medication, this could lead to a lawsuit. The chances of this happening, the senior hospital administrators had assured the board table, were likely. The family had been of no assistance. Mr. Rabini was unable to assume responsibility for his wife's care. He could not bring himself to force medication upon her if she didn't want it.

They were unable to convince him otherwise, despite the warnings of measures that would go into place to ensure his wife was not a menace to herself or others. The warnings fell on deaf ears.

The situation and its rhetoric had made Persey's head spin. She'd begun to feel sick to her stomach. She'd placed her hand over the bump in her abdomen, barely visible when she was naked and impossible to detect when she was clothed. She had not told the hospital that she was pregnant. She had not told anybody but Will. While in the meeting at the hospital, she had a sudden and violent spasm in her stomach. She had been suffering from morning sickness. She had moved her hand to cover her mouth, but the small amount of vomit that came up passed through her fingers and splashed onto the boardroom table.

She had stood and said, "Oh my God, please excuse me." She'd left the meeting.

Will sipped his coffee, then offered what comfort he could muster. He told her that the Indians used to leave the old and the infirm alone on islands in winter when they could no longer keep up with the migrations of the tribe.

"How did that heal them?" Persey asked.

"They were left there to die," Will said. "Every economy has boundaries on compassion."

"Indians," Persey said. "Fucking Indians."

QUEER LOVE

WILL AND PADDY SAT quietly in Paddy's bachelor apartment, watching *The Seven Samurai*. Will visited Paddy a few nights a week, mainly because he had begun to observe the smoking ban in Mrs. Duncan's rooming house.

Men frequently knocked on Paddy's door in the evenings. All kinds of men. Will assumed they were all on parole, like Cobb. Paddy told them to come back another time. Paddy did most of his work from home. He only went into the office a couple of times a week, to file reports and speak to his supervisor. Paddy was a good parole officer. His wards rarely went back to prison. They rarely reoffended. He told Will it was because he treated them like human beings.

Paddy had an exceptional VHS collection. He was something of a movie fanatic. He had hundreds and hundreds of television shows taped. He loved *Frasier*, and owned seven complete seasons. He was convinced Frasier was queer and didn't know it. Without a doubt, his favourite TV show was *Pee-wee Herman's Playhouse*. Will had watched hours and hours of Pee-wee with Paddy. It was a ritual for Paddy. He'd smoke a joint and watch Pee-wee Herman.

Throughout *The Seven Samurai*, Paddy interjected with factual information about homosexuality. Nanshoku, the love of the Samurai, or the Greek notion of the young acolyte and the elder mentor, played itself out in Paddy's semi-drunk and stoned ramblings. King sat beside him on the loveseat, his head resting on Paddy's lap. When the movie was over Paddy invited Will for a walk with King. Will agreed and they took the dog down to the lake.

The waves rolled in under the moonlight. Usually, King just urinated in the backyard of the building, but a few times a week Paddy liked to take him for a longer walk. It was not a daily occurrence, because King had bonded too well with Paddy and had the habit of growling and charging at strangers, especially in open spaces like the waterfront. He was a different dog at home, as Cobb had discovered. A handful of treats could pacify him — as they did on his occasional walks to the waterfront. It would have been cruel of Paddy not to take him for long walks, and Paddy wasn't cruel. Paddy always had a pocketful of treats with him.

The Samurai — at the peak of his prowess, after a life of solitude and practice, a life fixed on death, a death planned as meticulously as the most ostentatious of weddings — took a young lover. The young lover would bond with the older master, and thus the teachings of the Samurai were passed. The love channel, Paddy explained, is the best channel by which to receive difficult and sacred teachings. Japanese feudal society was guarded, protected and predicated upon the lives of homosexuals. The subtlest truths of the human race, the very foundation of the modern world, at least from the times of ancient Greece, were passed from generation to generation. This idea, haunting and warm to Paddy, was under the stars, which could be seen well by the lake, where the wind blew the pollution away. He gazed more and more upon the image of Will, which was more and more appealing to him. At first Paddy was disturbed. He tried to push the image away, but the boy had a certain beautiful presence.

It had been so long since Paddy had loved. There had been only one time really, and it had nearly destroyed him. Now it seemed that the possibility of reciprocated love was beyond him. He was fat and he was ugly. That was the simple truth. But then why had life thrown this beautiful boy into his path, this acolyte in the purest sense, true and innocent and beautiful? It was this beauty he wanted to protect from the world, from Parkdale, from anyone who would take it from him. It was the recognition of this beauty that incited deep feelings in Paddy, feelings he had not had for years. As King dumped on the grass before the shore, Paddy felt a wave of disgust. The very thought that he had been hiding from love for so long burst into him. He was barely even human anymore. He hadn't made love to a human being in years. He realized for the first time in a long time that he had mandated his own parole by the calcification of his feelings. He felt horrible with the realization.

Will was walking closer to the water. He returned to Paddy and King. They both stood and watched the waves and the sky.

Will asked, "Do you believe in God?"

Paddy looked at him and said, "Is God love?"

"I don't know. I think so."

Paddy said, "I believe in love."

There was a long silence. Then Paddy said, "You're a queer fellow, Will."

WARRIOR

WILL WAS WORKING ON some numbers in the attic. In the past week, Mr. Kenny at the bank had proposed the purchase of a small building with four apartments and a basement. It was a lovely old home that had been kept in beautiful condition. The owner was a Serb, who was liquidating assets before he submitted a financial statement to his wife's lawyer. Now was the time to move, Mr. Kenny had said. These were important decisions for William Tobe. In them lay his as-of-yet-unestablished status in the tribe of 1109897 Ontario Inc. Warrior.

Will and Cobb had $200,000 US in a Costa Rican bank account that had grown in less than four months from cash transfers. They had another $100,000 in the investment schedule Will had given the Royal Bank. Mr Kenny was fast becoming his best friend. They spoke three times a week on the phone, and they went to lunch together at least once a week. Robert Polski's portfolio was the largest monthly investment schedule Mr. Kenny's branch of the Royal Bank administered. After the first quarterly review, the numbers quadrupled. Mr. Kenny wanted to know more about the primary trust. Who was managing it? Will gave no details. The primary trust was between Cobb and him.

Mr. Kenny had done some elementary number crunching. He called Will into his office one day and they went over some charts and spreadsheets. He pointed out that the goal, in principle, upon the inception of their enterprise, had been to preserve half of Mr. Polski's wealth for his own expenses and investments and to invest half in safe short- and long-term returns. Will, in principle, agreed — the original numbers had been set at 55:45. The problem, as Mr. Kenny had defined it through his close observations, was that the incoming revenues, the dispersals from the primary trust, had been growing unabated at an almost unbelievable rate; therefore, to fulfill the original investment schedule, in principle, the automatic withdrawals had to be recalculated weekly. "And even that is only going to bring us to about 40:60," Mr. Kenny added, accounting, once again with genuine awe, for the unabated growth on the returns from the primary trust.

"But wouldn't that be too much work for the bank?" Will had asked.

"Oh, not at all, Mr. Tobe. That's what we're here for."

Will agreed and the whole enterprise was restructured. Mr. Kenny took full responsibility for the accounting. He also ensured the money transfers to Costa Rica, always in sums less than ten thousand. He wisely suggested they establish a corporate interest in Costa Rica and so, at the referral of Mr Kenny, Will contacted an elderly lawyer, *abrigado y notario*, named Miguel Sanchez in the small mountain village of Atenas. He became their agent in Costa Rica.

Sanchez was a lively old fellow who loved to talk on the telephone. He always began by describing what a beautiful day it was and how the sun had risen over the chapel in Atenas. He was a warm man. He had been a human rights lawyer in Nicaragua who had been forced to flee the country in the 1980s in fear for his life. Will was astonished to learn how cheap land was in Costa Rica. Miguel

Sanchez, *abrigado y notario*, explained that locals could not invest in their own economy because interest rates were prohibitive. The government could not or would not stabilize the currency. It was criminal, as far as he was concerned. He liked young William Tobe. He liked conservation investments in his country. Without them the whole country would go to land developers who could think of nothing but resorts and the profits they generated. Sanchez was an aggressive agent for 1109897 Ontario Inc. Will knew that Sanchez read the local papers every day for farm foreclosures and land auctions. Will had refused to make any purchases until he had analyzed the market for at least one quarter. Sanchez was on retainer. Central American property statistics were faxed to Will every day.

In the domestic market, Mr. Kenny's main ambition had been to free the ten percent allocated to the currencies fund and invest it in local commodities like small apartment buildings with low-maintenance costs and full tenancy. For every question Will raised, Mr. Kenny had an answer. It seemed as though his relationship with Robert Polski's portfolio was devotional. Even the name was whispered — Mr. Polski — as one with considerable capital accrues a higher status, regardless of whether the money was earned or inherited. Will gave Mr. Kenny the ten percent to work with, and they set up a side-bar agreement that made Mr. Kenny a commissioned consultant. Although Mr. Kenny held this title, he lacked signing authority without Will's, and hence Mr. Polski's, approval.

The warrior had become Will's spiritual goal. Cobb had told him that only someone with courage could find meaning in a vision. Will continued to take his long walking meditations when he could, but Cobb kept him quite busy. He wasn't giving Will's salary away. They had a lot of meetings. Sometimes Robert Polski was there. Sometimes he wasn't. Cobb was increasingly interested in the history, philosophy and workings of the modern economy. Cobb and Will had spent many hours cross-legged in the attic, going over the photocopies of Mr. Kenny's graphs and spreadsheets. They spoke their own language. They called the secured capital "dream money" and Cobb realized quickly that dream money could only be invested in a dream economy. Will always felt that he was very well taken care of by Cobb. There was no question. He had more pocket money than most lawyers, yet questions about status crept into his mind. Nobody could be completely comfortable until he knows his place. Cobb told him that he was a coureur-de-bois, a runner of the woods. They were the first white men to work with the Indians in Canada, and to do so they broke the King of France's rules. Cobb gave Will his blessing to manage the dream money as he dreamed fit, though he insisted that he be made aware of all transactions before they took place. Cobb was happy with the seed Will was sowing in the fields above the earth. The young William Tobe seemed to have been given a vision of the dream economy. He knew where he was going. His vision had given him a map of unknown places. If his dream fields reaped a good harvest there would be a division of the common shares. Equity was a powerful incentive for Will, and it answered his questions about status. Cobb had given his vision a quest. It would define his status.

The telephone rang down on the landing of Cobb's floor, the second floor. Will wasn't sure if Cobb was home. He thought that he had heard footsteps coming up the stairs, a door slam, but he couldn't be sure. There was no rush. He didn't have to run down the stairs from the attic. He had set the answering machine to nine rings before it picked up. It drove a lot of people crazy, but it was the only way he could get to every call and, as Cobb never answered the phone, he had to get every call.

The telephone was on a small end table at the foot of the stairs leading up to the attic. The stairs were very steep and had to be taken slowly. By the fifth ring he was at the phone.

"Hello," he said.

It was for Cobb.

"I don't know anything about any peyote," Will said into the phone, "but I'll have Cobb call you back." He took the message and hung up.

Just as he was about to stand and ascend the stairs, he heard a moan from the kitchen. The kitchen was on the other side of the wall. He thought he was hearing things so he sat very still. He heard it again, a woman's low moan and then a muffled giggle, as though it came from behind a hand. Will stood and walked around the corner and into the kitchen.

Cobb was buck naked, his penis inside a blond woman who was bent over the kitchen table, and there appeared to be another woman, a brunette, behind Cobb. She was licking his behind.

"Who was that on the phone?" Cobb asked without interrupting his activity.

"Some guy named Philmore."

Cobb nodded his head.

"You have any idea what's making that banana smell?" Cobb asked, and the brunette girl pulled back from Cobb's behind and said, "Bananas," two or three times, then laughed hysterically.

"I don't have a clue," Will said and he turned and left. But he stopped at the foot of the stairs and asked, "Do we want a building with four apartments and an unfinished basement ... private sale?"

"Full market value?" Cobb said from the kitchen.

"I'd say about seventy percent," Will said.

"Fuck yeah," Cobb answered.

Will started up the stairs.

"Oh," Cobb said, "there's a message from your girlfriend on the phone. She sounds like she's going to kill herself."

"She's not my girlfriend," Will responded from the attic, and with that statement he shut his door.

HATCHET

Cobb's sessions with Dr. Bluette had degenerated to him regaling her with stories from his youth on the reserve. Dr. Bluette couldn't get enough of "Indian lore." He had already told her all about his mother, her abandonment of him and her subsequent death. Dr. Bluette was extremely sympathetic. In Cobb she found the fulfillment she had always craved from her profession. She could take her practice to another world, and she could heal. Cobb took none of the drugs she prescribed. He sold them all on the street. Every second session Dr. Bluette would ask how the medication was working. Cobb would shrug his shoulders and say that he still felt a little down or unable to sleep or prone to bursts of anger and for these symptoms there was always a prescription. On top of the prescriptions Dr. Bluette wrote, Cobb got more drugs by tearing a few sheets off her prescription pad every time he was left alone in her office for a minute or two. He had mastered her script and could forge her signature so well she wouldn't be able to tell the difference.

On this day, Cobb was telling Dr. Bluette about the work he and his grandfather used to do during the bear hunts.

"It's usually an American," Cobb said with a sardonic drawl and a wink. Dr. Bluette disliked Americans and Cobb was not above playing to a person's preferences. "They talk a lot about guns and being armed, but all we wanted on the reserve was for them to learn how to shoot."

Dr. Bluette laughed a little laugh. She was sitting at her desk, her head resting against one of her palms, a restrained smile on her face. She looked forward to her meetings with Cobb.

"Me and Grandpa would never get word of a wounded bear until evening, a couple hours after dinner. The first time I went with him I was eleven years old. I had a hatchet and he had a hatchet. We would get in his pickup truck and drive to where the hunters came out of the bush. Now, the hunt guide should have been able to kill the bear, but he was just some university guy with a degree in biology. That's not tracking. The guy ran bait lines all through the bush. He knew where the bears were because their food chains had been set up by him. If hunters came up from the US and they hadn't seen a bear after three days in the bush, this guide would blowtorch honey in a fry pan. That would bring the bears running. They love honey." Cobb winked when he said honey.

"So what you do then, is you set out at dusk, and you track the bear with nothing more than a flashlight and moonlight. You can't wait until morning. A wounded bear is too dangerous. The hardest part about the job was getting one of the hunters to go back into the bush with you to show you where the blood trail starts. They were too scared. Wounding a bear strikes a deep fear in most people."

"Why do you think that is?" Dr. Bluette asked.

"Maybe they know it's close to killing a person, and they feel bad."

Dr. Bluette nodded her head. "I never would have thought of that."

"So you get to the blood trail. Sometimes it's big and sometimes it's small. If it's small you have to watch the leaves, the branches, and the forest floor closely. It's hard for a wounded bear to cover its tracks. Well, it's hard for any bear to cover its tracks, but a wounded bear is also leaving a blood trail. So then you follow the blood trail by moonlight. Sometimes it takes only a little while. Other times you can still be tracking well into the next day."

"You don't go home and sleep?" Dr. Bluette asked.

"Nope," Cobb said. "Can't. Bear's gotta be killed. No telling what a wounded bear can do."

Dr. Bluette nodded her head.

"This time, me and Grandpa tracked till dawn, then we came to a small clearing. You have to stop and get your bearings in a clearing. Find out which way the bear went. The blood trail was small. Grandpa said the bear was still strong. You gotta be real careful with a slightly wounded bear. They're really angry and still strong and fast."

Dr. Bluette raised her eyebrows and let her mouth hang open.

"So me and Grandpa kneeled down to look at the ground for prints. It took Grandpa about two minutes to figure out that the bear had turned around. You see," Cobb said, "the bear had decided to track us."

"Do they do that a lot?" Dr. Bluette asked.

"It's not unheard of," Cobb said. "The bear came out of the bush behind us and charged me. I was only fourteen at the time."

"Fourteen years old?" Dr. Bluette said.

"Yeah, fourteen. Anyhow, the bear came at me. The last thing I remember seeing were those two eyes. They were so human."

"What happened?" Dr. Bluette asked.

"My grandfather told me the bear swiped at me and that I was thrown about ten feet against a tree. It was a big bear, over four hundred pounds."

"You were knocked unconscious?" Dr. Bluette asked.

"Yeah, but I got my hatchet into its heart before it hit me. Grandpa came in and gave it the finishing blow."

"Why didn't you take a rifle with you?"

"Grandpa thought it wasn't a fair way for a noble creature to die, also because when they charge you don't have time to get a rifle shot off."

"My God, I don't know what I would do if a bear ever charged me."

"You'd do what you had to," Cobb said. "It's in you. All the really important stuff is just in us. It doesn't have to be taught."

Dr. Bluette smiled and looked at her watch. "Well, that's about it for today, Randall. How are you feeling?"

"I got angry with my boss the other day. I wanted to tear his head off."

"What did he do?" Dr. Bluette asked.

"He had a better lunch than me."

"Excuse me?" Dr. Bluette said.

"He had a meatball sub his wife made. I just had processed cheese slices on white bread."

"I see," Dr. Bluette said. "Are you still taking the Zolfax?"

"Yep."

"And the sedatives?"

"Yep."

"I see," Dr. Bluette said. She wrote out a prescription and handed it to Cobb. "Try this, too," she said.

"Thanks," Cobb said.

"Your parole is concluded in a few months, Randall. If you want to continue with our work here, I can arrange it. No expense to you."

"I'll see what Paddy says."

Dr. Bluette smiled. "You two have become quite close, haven't you?"

"He really cares," Cobb said.

"I know," Dr. Bluette said. "They tried to get rid of him a few years ago. One of his wards told Canada Corrections that he was drunk at every appointment."

"He's like a wounded bear in the justice system," Cobb said.

Cobb smiled. He was pleased with himself.

EARLY SNOW

WILL AND PERSEY WALKED down by the lake. It was cold, not winter cold, fall cold, but cold nonetheless because their blood was still thin from the warm weather that had proceeded the sudden cold. Sudden weather turns had become common. Will had looked into the phenomenon. Some said it was the greenhouse gases. Others said it was a natural climate change, that the earth went through phases of heating up and cooling down. On some web sites, self-taught meteorologists and conspiracy theorists warned of catastrophic events, and there was division among the highly politicized scientific community, which was, in fact, what Will and Persey were talking about walking along the lakeshore that cold evening.

"The most important science is the least understood," Will said. "Economics is our foundation science. No other science is possible without it."

"Okay," Persey said, nodding her head as they walked slowly in front of waves that rolled in, bushed by the cold wind that came off the lake.

"The whole point of science is certainty, but it's a relatively young practice in our history. The last hundred years have been the biggest leap forward in known human history, throwing out the Atlantis and Lemuria advocates. We know of no other age that lived with the kind of technology we do."

"Right," Persey said.

"So how can you have some scientists saying there's no problem with greenhouse gases and others saying we've reached the eleventh hour with fossil fuels? It makes no sense."

"And you should see medicine," Persey piped in. "They produce these drugs in beta form and give them to people as human guinea pigs."

"It's an economy where a single force controls both supply and demand. It's not a legitimate construct." Will paused and looked out over the water. "Never in the history of our species have we been more developed, and never in our history has the future of our species been more dire. We can't or won't see four generations into the future. At least the Indians could guarantee the earth for their children. We can't even do that."

"Indians?" Persey said.

"Natural economists," Will said.

They walked in silence for a few moments, then Persey's cellphone rang.

"Hello? Yes. In a little while. Yes, Mother. No. What? No. Goodbye." Persey ended the phone call.

"My mother would like to meet you."

Will became aware of something on his arm. It wasn't rain. He looked into the darkening sky. It was snowing. The snow was beginning to fall over Lake Ontario.

PISS IN A CUP

"COBB SAYS THAT THE federal corrections system suffers from systemic corruption. He says that all the guards are related at Warkworth. Cobb says the prison guards commit more crimes on a daily basis than all of the crimes of the inmates added together. Cobb says the guards run the tuck shop for the prisoners, and that the prisoners have to buy all their stuff, like shoes and toothpaste, from the prison tuck shop. Cobb says the guards go and buy shoes for $35 at a department store and then sell them to the prisoners for $129. And get this, Cobb says they collect the goods and services tax from the prisoners and then don't turn it over to the government. Cobb says that if the Auditor General's office had its staff tripled, a lot of civil servants would go to jail in this country. Cobb says the union has this work policy that everyone plays at. He says the guards call in sick a couple of times a week, and then someone has to cover for them, and that person gets paid double time for working an unscheduled shift. That's the way the union negotiated it. Then, the guy who called in sick at the beginning of the week tells the shift supervisor he feels a lot better at the end of the week, and that if anyone calls in sick he's available for an unscheduled shift, and, of course, he gets paid double time for it, and, of course, his buddy that covered for him at the beginning of the week calls in sick at the end of the week." Will looked for a response from Paddy, who was fixing himself a rye and ginger. He had a joint lit in his free hand. "Are you sure you don't want a drink?" Paddy asked. His back was to Will. He had on his pink housecoat over his boxer shorts, and he had rabbit-ear slippers on his feet.

"Why don't you take a hit off this joint? What's with this squeaky clean stuff, anyway? I'm starting to wonder if you're a narc."

"I can't drink or use drugs, Paddy. You know that. I've told you that."

Paddy shook his head, picked up his drink and returned to his seat.

"Cobb says that the prison system is constantly claiming it has no money, that it has to close down programs, and Cobb says a good portion of the money in the prison budgets is being siphoned off by corrupt unions and fraudulent bookkeeping."

"Will," Paddy said, pausing deliberately for a moment, his eyes looking up and away, "I want you to understand something. Prison is a very difficult environment, with very many stresses. Most convicts come out of jail with attitudes very similar to Cobb's. You just need to see that it's anger that's colouring their perception, and where there is coloured perception, there is false reporting. Do you want to understand what I'm trying to tell you?"

"I think so."

"Good," Paddy said, "because you've taken on quite a responsibility living with Cobb. You have to be part of his rehabilitative process. You're young, and you're full of hope and goodness. Yes," Paddy said when Will lifted his face to look at him. "Goodness. I see goodness in you. Just give Cobb his space. He has a lot of anger to work through."

"Cobb says you can tell good people from bad people by how they treat vulnerable things."

"Well, that's probably true," Paddy said, "but do I need to remind you, Will, that your friend is a convicted felon? That means he has burdened society with the costs of his incarceration, not to mention the cost of his trial. Destructive behaviour ripples through our whole society, Will, and it affects us all, not least of all in the taxes we pay."

Will stubbed his cigarette in the ashtray. He buttoned up his coat. It was cold outside. It was that time of year right between fall and winter. The cold with its immovable persistence was almost there. It had already snowed.

"Oh," Will said. "I almost forgot. Here are your cigarettes." Will handed Paddy the carton of cigarettes. He frowned a little and said, "Listen, I'm almost embarrassed to bring this up, but Cobb says you have to think about settling your tab pretty soon."

"What's it at?" Paddy asked.

"Just shy of $400," Will said.

"Ouch," Paddy said. "That's a big cigarette tab."

"Cobb says you haven't paid for weeks."

"Okay," Paddy said. "Tell Cobb I'll settle up in the middle of the month."

"That should be all right," Will said.

"I'm out of weed, too," Paddy said, almost asking.

"Cobb says no more weed until the tab is paid."

Paddy looked forlorn for a moment. "That's a bit extreme, don't you think?"

"I don't know," Will said. "Oh," Will added, pulling a sample jar from his coat pocket, "Here's Cobb's urine sample."

Paddy said, "I'm supposed to witness the urine test if he doesn't go to a designated clinic."

"Come on, Paddy," Will said, "I'm not going to let you watch me piss in a cup."

PART FOUR

WINTER

STREAM

SOMETHING PACIFIC HELD THE night together. The first thought that came to Will was that it was the time, the season, but it didn't stay. It slipped into the night and no other thoughts replaced it, so he accepted the peace. There were a few patches of white left but most of the snow had melted. The grey clouds that had been visible during the day and had brought the snow in the late afternoon rested between the street and the night, invisible but perceptible because they hid the stars. The two- and three-storey brick buildings were wet, as was the ground, and the air was cold. "Every vision is the responsibility of its seer," Cobb said.

"I'm not asking you to interpret my vision," Will said. "I'm just asking you to help me understand if it even was a vision."

Cobb thought about the request for a moment and said, "A vision is like an erection. It's a part of you but not really a part of you. It seems to have its own life."

"A hard-on?" Will said.

"We have to wait a few minutes," Cobb said. "Give them a head start."

"What do they look like?" Will asked.

"Not too bad," Cobb said. "Not too fucking bad."

Cobb and Will stood on the sidewalk for five minutes and said nothing, then they started to walk down the street. It was 1109897 Ontario Inc.'s executive Christmas party, but it was just Will and Cobb. Robert Polski hadn't been seen for quite some time. He had just sort of disappeared. They weren't worried. Polski made his own way in the world. He answered to nobody. Cobb and Will respected him for it. He was their absent chief. It was the twenty-third of December, just past the shortest day of the year, and winter by any calendar.

They turned into the tavern at the Gladstone Hotel. There were two men at the one pool table in the tavern, the only other patrons aside from Will, Cobb and two prostitutes, who were sitting at the bar. Cobb and Will went over and sat on either side of them. The bartender walked over, stopped in front of Cobb and pointed at the drinks in front of the prostitutes. Cobb threw a ten dollar bill down. The bartender scooped it up, ambled back to the cash register, opened and closed it, then ambled back to Cobb, dropped his change on the bar and went back to the far end where he had been reading a newspaper.

The prostitutes tipped their glasses and held them tipped until just the ice was rattling against their teeth. They got off their stools and walked to the lobby without indicating whether Cobb and Will were to follow them. Cobb got up and motioned for Will to do the same. The bartender never looked out from behind his newspaper. On the way out to the lobby, Will saw Dorothy, the waitress from the Dolphin, in a dark corner of the tavern. She pretended not to see him. When Cobb and Will got into the lobby they caught sight of the two black skirts as they disappeared around the corner to ascend the second flight of stairs. Cobb and Will followed, always a flight of stairs behind the prostitutes until the fourth floor, which was the last. Cobb opened the door to the landing, which had one mirrored bureau with a black rotary telephone on it and one tin garbage can with no lid. The landing smelled of sour milk.

"Shit, this place stinks worse than the bathroom at home," Cobb snickered, as though he enjoyed the smell despite his complaint.

When they turned the corner and could see down the hall, the prostitutes were at the end of the hall looking back at them.

Cobb turned to Will and said, "Okay, which one do you want?"

Will didn't look down the hall. He looked at the floor instead.

"It doesn't matter to me."

He felt a movement in his stomach and winced.

"Okay," Cobb said. "I'll take the shorter one."

Cobb nodded his head, more to himself than Will, then he started down the hall. Will grabbed his elbow.

"What does the tall one look like up close?"

"She's okay," Cobb said. "She's okay."

"All right," Will said.

They both walked down the hall. Will noticed that the floor wasn't level and that most of the doors had been poorly cut to their frames. He caught glimpses of the life inside some of the rooms, shadows, light thrown from a television screen, an old man in an undershirt. He heard voices from the rooms.

"Hey, *It's a Wonderful Life* is on television," Will said. His face glowed with childlike warmth.

"It's a good flick," Cobb said. "I saw it this week at Paddy's. He has it on tape."

Each of the prostitutes had a hand on a doorknob and they were facing each other with their backs against the two doors on opposite sides of the hall. Cobb directed himself toward the shorter, younger woman. She opened the door and the two of them went into the room. Cobb shut the door behind them. Will and the other prostitute were left in the hall alone. A long moment passed before Cobb reappeared.

"Almost forgot," he said.

He handed the older woman some rolled up bills. She clenched the money in her fist and went into her room. She left the door open behind her.

Cobb looked at Will and said, "Every moment we're living we're dying," and then he went back into his room.

Will went into the room his woman had gone into and closed the door behind him.

The tall woman appeared about thirty-five to Will and the cheekbones which had made her look exotic in the bad lighting of the bar left her frail-looking under the room's one bare light bulb in the centre of the twelve-foot-high ceiling. Will stood just inside the room with his back to the door. He watched her clear off the bed, which had a bag of overripe bananas on it, a garbage bag full of clothes and a few CDs. He saw that her skin was blotched with pink marks and the veins in her thin forearms were as pronounced as the grooves in a coarse bark. Her lips were hard and chapped in spots. Her nose was pointed. Her eyes were dark and sunken. Her hair was black at the roots. The room had a queen-size bed on an old steel frame, a large cabinet with a mirrored door, a clothes bureau, a television, a small, empty bookcase, a round table with two chairs by a window that overlooked a parking lot and the railway bridge that crossed over the street Will and Cobb had just walked up. As Will looked around the room he could sense a profound feeling of vacancy, despite all the articles crammed into it. Looking up he realized it was the high ceiling that gave him the feeling.

"So, what do you do?" the prostitute asked.

"I manage an investment portfolio in a small corporation that wants to get into the oxygen market before it's fully defined. That takes up a good portion of my time. And I had a vision that I'm trying to understand."

"Unh-huh," the prostitute said. "So what do you want, baby?"

She stood on the other side of the bed with her hands on her hips. Will shrugged his shoulders.

"You don't know?" she said. "Would you like me to suck you?"

Will nodded his head.

"All right, take your pants off then."

Will unbuttoned his jeans and let them fall to his ankles, then he sat down, unlaced his shoes, took them off, pulled his jeans over his feet and threw them into a corner of the room.

"Your underwear, too," she said. "You can leave the socks on. It's kind of cold in here."

He looked into her eyes then bent his head down, pushed his jockey shorts to his feet and kicked them into the corner with his jeans.

"Do you want to take your shirt off, baby?" she asked from where she sat on the bed with her legs curled under her like a cat.

He unbuttoned his shirt and tossed it into the corner, then stared at her from his seat at the little table by the window.

She got off the bed and walked over to him slowly, removing her black blouse, fetishizing each button in a practised eroticism. She had on a black bra, which she unclasped and let fall to the floor. Her breasts were small. He cupped one. It was firm. The nipple stayed soft and fleshy as he pinched it gently between his index finger and thumb.

"What's your name?" he asked her.

"Candy," she said.

"How do you spell it?"

"C-A-N-D-Y."

She got on her knees and leaned in between his legs, which she spread further apart with her hands, and she began licking his soft penis. He felt a stir between his legs but didn't get hard. She kept licking and looking up at him every fifteen seconds or so.

"I don't want to take it into my mouth," she said. "Even though you're not really hard yet you could still shoot. As soon as you get a little harder I'll put a safe on it."

He didn't really hear her. His eyes were closed. He heard the cars passing under the railway bridge and the one short train that crossed over the bridge. Her voice melded into these noises and was as meaningless.

"Are you going to help me here, baby?" she asked from between his legs.

"What?" he said.

"You've got to help me here, baby."

"How?"

"You're not getting hard."

"Sorry."

"Don't be sorry. Just get hard." She bent back in and began anew to lick his still soft penis. After another minute of licking and kissing she looked up with a frustrated and impatient face. Her lips were pursed and the callous parts were white.

"What do you want me to do?" she asked.

"I don't know," he answered.

"What if I play with myself and you see if you can get your cock hard? Play with it while you watch me. Then we'll throw a safe on it and you can put it in me, all right?"

She wiggled her bony hips while pushing on her black skirt, which fell from her knees to the ground as she sat back and slid into the centre of the bed. She pulled aside the crotch of her black panties with the fingers of her left hand, then, with her right hand, began to stroke the lips of her vagina, all the while staring fixedly at him and trying to hold a seductive grin that had to be loosened every few seconds to relieve the strain on the hard dry parts of her lips. As she stroked he noticed that the pink glitter nail polish was chipped on all her nails.

"Take hold of your cock, baby," she said.

Will didn't move.

"What's the matter, baby?"

"I don't know."

A moment of confusion crossed over her face before the sexual melodrama she had created retreated back into and behind her eyes, then she bounced off the bed with a speed that alarmed him and fumbled on the floor for her skirt, her bra, and her blouse.

"You're not getting a cent back," she said.

She pulled her skirt back on.

"I know," Will said.

"I can't give you a fucking cent back, baby. For all I know this is your trip and then you just go home and whack yourself off, either way you've used me and I can't give you a cent back." She slid her arms into her blouse and buttoned it up.

"I know," Will said. "It's no problem."

"What are you going to tell your friend?" she asked. Will could tell that she was afraid of Cobb.

He knew then that it was just her and her friend. Nobody was looking after them. They alone had to get out of whatever they got into.

"Nothing," Will said. "It's none of his business."

Some of the tension slipped out of her body when he said this. She slowed the frantic pace at which she had been dressing. She slipped her feet into her black pumps and sat down on the edge of the bed.

"You better stay a few minutes so you don't look stupid in front of your friend."

"Fuck him," Will said.

She smiled.

"You two aren't friends?" she asked.

"Yes. He's my best friend right now. We live in the same rooming house. I just mean that if I stay it's because I want to stay for a few minutes, not because I'm worried about what my friend is going to think."

"Do you want to hear some music?" she asked.

"Sure. Yes," Will said.

She got a radio from the cabinet and handed Will the cord.

"Can you plug this in behind the table," she said.

Will took the cord and plugged it in. They sat without speaking for several minutes and listened to pop music on the clock radio. She let one of her heels slip so that it was dangling from her toes, and she swayed her foot to the rhythm so that the bed frame began to creak and it, too, sounded like a part of the harmony. She reached back and pulled a large deck of cards out from under one of the pillows.

"The room doesn't seem so empty with the music," Will said. "When I first came in it seemed so empty because the ceiling is so high, but the music seems to fill it up somehow."

He watched her look through the cards.

"Yeah," she said. "These old hotels have really high ceilings. I like them like that."

She dug out a pack of cigarettes from under a pillow on the bed and offered him one, "Cigarette?"

"Thanks," Will said, and held out two fingers.

She slipped a cigarette between them. He lit it with a book of matches that was on the table then held the match out for her.

"Thank you," she said.

They sat quietly again and listened to the music, and after a few minutes she began to sway her foot again.

"Are you staying in town for Christmas?" she asked.

"Yes. Cobb, my buddy, he's going northeast, but I'm staying."

"What are you going to do?"

"I don't know. Just bum around, I guess. See a few movies."

"You don't have any family here?"

"No. None."

She held out the open pack of cigarettes.

"Take one for the road," she said. "Your friend is probably finished."

"Thanks," Will said. "What are those cards?" he asked, pointing to the cards she had brought out.

"These? They're tarot cards."

"Can you do that? Read them?"

"Sure."

"How?"

"My mother taught me."

"How did she learn?"

"It's not too hard. I could teach you. But being good at it is a little harder."

"What do they do?"

"They tell you things."

"What kinds of things?"

"Anything, a fact, a feeling — the future. They bring everything into focus."

"How does it work?"

"It just works."

"Like how?"

"It connects the stream inside you with the stream outside you, and for a while you get to stop moving."

"Read mine," Will said.

"Now?"

"Yes."

"I have to charge you."

"What about the money my friend gave you for the sex?"

"That's expired, honey. It's not my fault you didn't do anything with the time you had."

"How much for a reading?"

"It's usually forty, but I'll give it to you for thirty."

"All right," Will said.

"Do you believe in the cards?"

"See, there you go, I have to believe, right? I have to believe."

"Not totally, but it helps."

"How can it be real if I have to believe it?"

She didn't say anything.

"Ah, fuck it," Will said, and picked up his jacket, left the room and went down to the bar to wait for Cobb.

After Will had had a beer and the other cigarette Candy had given him, Cobb came into the bar. They had a beer together then Cobb handed him a Christmas card with a promissory note for half the common shares in 1109897 Ontario Inc. The note was legitimate. It was signed by Robert Polski. Cobb refused to say where he had found him, saying only, "Robert Polski wants to be alone." Will and Cobb were now full partners.

CHARLIE BROWN CHRISTMAS

It was dark when Will left his room on Christmas Eve. The street was deserted and white. The air was sharp on his lips and throat and gusts turned sporadically, unsettling the snowdrifts that had accumulated in the corners of driveways. An empty streetcar passed like a ghost and Will listened to its grinding grow faint. He had not noticed from his window that the Dolphin was closed, the first time he had seen it so before last call. The hanging unlit neon sign and the dark emptiness of the interior seemed an absurdity to him. A middle-aged man passed with two small dogs and nodded a greeting, to which Will said, "Merry Christmas," wondering where the man had appeared from so suddenly.

The lights in the basement hall of Paddy's building had been burnt out for a week. It was almost pitch black except for the cut of light under Paddy's door. Will heard no noise inside but, accustomed to this, knocked twice, to which the immediate response was, "Come in."

Will entered and fell into the sofa. Paddy had videotaped *A Charlie Brown Christmas* and was watching it. Charlie Brown picked the frailest, ugliest tree on the lot. Paddy started howling and slapping his knee.

"You think that's funny?" Will said.

"What?"

"Charlie Brown."

"Not him, Linus, he's the only one who isn't against Charlie Brown." Paddy took a sip of his rye and ginger. "Mind you, he's not for him either."

"You kind of remind me of Charlie Brown, Paddy."

"You kind of remind me of Linus. Maybe we should be syndicated."

They watched the show until the credits began to roll, then Paddy got up and put on *How the Grinch Stole Christmas*. Paddy fell into the loveseat again and looked generally peaceful, the way he did on Sundays when Will showed up at his place before he'd had his first four cups of coffee. It was in moments like this that Will came to a deeper understanding of Paddy, of how vulnerable he was. Paddy was an easy target for ridicule. His appearance alone was enough to spark interest in the mean-spirited; and if he spoke it furthered his vulnerability to the ill-willed. Dorothy, the waitress at the Dolphin, hated him. Kids on the street laughed at him. In moments like this Will saw the courage with which Paddy lived his circumstance, the commitment he had made to himself. He had acquired the ability to imbue the plainest of moments with meaning, if only in the way he accented it. He was always acutely aware of other people's toils. Will thought of Paddy as royalty in that moment, a benign monarch in a malignant kingdom, the queen of King Street.

"Linus is a realist and Charlie Brown is a dreamer," Paddy said.

"I don't know," Will said. "I'd have to give that some thought."

"Please do," Paddy said.

Will looked closely at Paddy.

"What are you doing?" Paddy asked.

"I was just noticing how beautiful you are."

TARIFF

Will and Robert were making cigarette deliveries. They got out of the truck on King Street and grabbed their smokes from the back of the pickup. Robert liked to go on the cigarette run once in a while — if he caught Will early in the morning having breakfast at the Dolphin. Polski had been gone for weeks and weeks, then he just appeared again. He'd bought himself some new clothes. Life was a little easier for him with the money Cobb and Will gave him.

When they entered the store, Mr. Chow was behind the cash register. It was always either him or his wife. He had raised three kids in Canada. He didn't really need to work anymore. He spoke a lot about selling his convenience store, but there was little chance that was going to happen. He couldn't think of anything else to do with his time. Going back to China was on his mind, but then he'd have a legion of relatives knocking on his door with requests for money. The place he came from was quite poor, not one of China's special economic zones.

Will noticed right away that there was something wrong. Mr. Chow had a worried and apprehensive look about him. Before Will could inquire, a huge man came out of one of the aisles of the convenience store. He had a long brown beard and long brown hair. Will guessed he was close to three hundred pounds. He wore a leather jacket and there were tattoos on his neck.

"You the cigarette guy?" he asked, walking right up to Will and towering over him.

"Pardon?" Will said.

The man lifted his arm and poked Will in the chest with a big finger.

"I said, are you the cigarette guy?"

"Who's asking?" Will said.

The man leaned down and whispered into Will's ear.

"Oh," Will said. His face lost all colour.

"We want a piece," the man said. "Protection."

"Well, I'm not really the boss," Will said.

The man backhanded Will and Will flew into the counter in front of Mr. Chow.

"No. No. No. No," Mr. Chow said. "No violence in store."

The man walked over and picked Will up with one hand and started to drag him out of the store.

Before he could get to the front door, he collapsed to the ground, a red liquid all over the cheaply tiled floor around him. Robert Polski was standing behind the man's unconscious form with another glass jar of Ragu spaghetti sauce cocked and ready to go, just in case the first didn't do the job.

"Jesus, Robert," Will said.

"Must go now," Mr. Chow said.

Will bent down and fished the man's wallet out. He took a motorcycle licence from the wallet and left with Robert, after Mr. Chow paid for his cigarettes.

They got into the truck and drove away, not knowing how long the man in Mr. Chow's store would be unconscious.

"Thanks, Robert," Will said as he dialled Cobb's cellphone.

Robert smiled and nodded his head.

Cobb answered on the fourth ring.

"Yeah."

"Cobb, Will. Big trouble. Robert knocked out a —"

"Not on the phone," Cobb said. He told Will where he was and to come and get him.

A short while later Will pulled to the side of the road and Cobb came out of a Vietnamese acrylic nail and cosmetics shop. Cobb opened the passenger door and a burst of cold air chilled Will and Robert. He squeezed into the cab of the truck and Will drove away. Will explained as he drove. Cobb said nothing. When Will was finished, he said, "Robert, we have to drop you off at the hotel now. Don't come out until we come and get you. It might take until tomorrow."

"Okay," Robert said.

They dropped Robert off and then drove out of the city a few hours, to a reserve north of Toronto. Cobb got out of the truck and told Will to wait. Fifteen minutes passed before the back of the truck opened and Cobb loaded in two pit bulls. They immediately ran to the front of the truck and rammed their heads against the glass in an attempt to get at Will. Cobb slammed the door shut. He slid back into the cab of the truck. He told Will to drive back to the city. Will drove off the reserve and back onto the highway. They drove in silence for a while, then Will said, "What's the plan?"

Cobb stroked his smooth chin. "What would an economist do?"

"It's clearly a trade dispute," Will said. "They want a tariff."

"A tariff?"

"Yes," Will said. "The modern economy is doing away with tariffs. That's what free trade is all about. This is King-of-France shit. It's an open market. We don't owe them anything."

"They're selling protection," Cobb said.

"Protection? From what?" Will asked.

"From them," Cobb said.

"What are we going to do?"

"I have to make a few calls," Cobb said, and he did just that. He made a half dozen phone calls within an hour, and then he spoke to Will.

"Guy wasn't patched. He's just a prospect. I gotta go for a sit down."

"A sit down? What's that?" Will asked.

"I go. I sit. I talk. It's a negotiation," Cobb said.

"Are we going to give them a percentage?"

"No fucking way," Cobb said. The dogs growled in the back. Cobb slammed his hand against the glass and the dogs yelped and ran to the back of the truck.

"Do I have to go in?" Will asked.

"Nope," Cobb said. "I go in alone." Cobb looked out the window into the dark woods beside the highway. "Tariffs, eh?"

Will was nervous; he started talking non-stop. He told Cobb that tariffs were everywhere in human history, that economics had to reflect human nature, despite ideals and intentions. The Silk Road to China was lined with brigands and cutthroats. The American Revolution was about tariffs imposed through the British Crown. Early on, the English had perfected the duplicitous art of trading. Will told Cobb that when they ran out of gold they traded opium for tea and strung out a good portion of China because the English loved their tea. Will worked his way to the near present and explained free trade and hemispheric trading blocks to Cobb, telling him about the soft wood lumber disputes between Canada and the US. Then Will went further. He told Cobb his theories on original sin and karma, the debt a person is born under, and how even that seemed evidence of an economy run by God, and finally, as Cobb directed Will to their destination, a concrete-fortified bungalow with bars on its windows in the southeast end of the city, Will talked about prison and madness as the two final and most extreme forms of tariff, one leaving a person behind bars and the other leaving a person medicated, shocked or in a straight jacket.

"Protection from themselves?" Cobb asked.

"I guess," Will said, and he put the truck in park a half block from the bungalow and left the engine idling to keep the heat.

"Have you come to understand your vision yet?" Cobb asked.

"No," Will said.

Cobb opened the glove box and took out a piece of paper and a pen. He wrote a phone number and a name: Tom Tom.

"If I don't come out in fifteen minutes, call this number."

Will said nothing. He nodded.

Cobb reached under the passenger seat of the truck cab and pulled out a short wood-handled hatchet, which he tucked into the back of his pants, under his jacket. He nodded once at Will and got out of the truck. Will watched him walk to the door, setting off motion-sensitive floodlights in front the bungalow. Cobb knocked. An eye-level hatch slid back in the metal door, then the door opened. Cobb entered the house. The door closed behind him.

A horrible fear set itself in William Tobe. A large rat crawled around in his stomach. His head felt worse. His leg bounced up and down uncontrollably. He looked like an addict in withdrawal. He turned on the radio. The radio announcer said, "Here's a tune that never loses its time," and then John Lennon's "Imagine" started.

The song calmed him. When it was over he switched the radio off and picked up Cobb's cellphone. The dashboard clock said that Cobb had been in the house six minutes. He dialled a long distance number. A man answered.

"Hello."

"Dad — "

"Will?"

"Yes —"

"What the hell's going on, Will? You disappear without a word. Your sister thinks you've had some kind of breakdown —"

"Dad —"

"— your mother's been worried sick —"

"Dad —"

"— and what about school? Did we discuss a sabbatical? You're not on your own here, Will. We've invested a lot of time and money in —"

"Dad —"

"What?"

"I love you, Dad."

"Will, is everything all right?"

"Everything is fine, Dad. I'll be back to school next year."

"What's this all about, Will?"

"I just needed some time off."

"I want you to call home and say hello to your mother. She's not in right now."

"I'll call tomorrow."

"You're sure everything is all right?"

"Couldn't be better, Dad."

"Why don't you come home, spend some time with us."

"I have a business to run ... Bye, Dad."

Will ended the phone call. Cobb had been in the house eight minutes. In another seven minutes Will would have to make another phone call, then a tribe of Mohawks would descend on this fortified bungalow. How did it all come to this? he wondered. He took a deep breath and closed his eyes. He started to pray. He moved his lips and nodded his head slightly. This went on until the passenger door to the truck pulled open and Cobb poked his head into the cab.

"It's all good," he said. "I'll be back in five minutes." He closed the door and went to the back of the truck. He took the dogs out and walked back to the front of the house. The door opened again and again Cobb disappeared inside. The clock on the dashboard said that fourteen minutes had passed.

Cobb came out almost immediately, but without the dogs. He walked briskly to the truck, opened the passenger door and climbed in.

"I smoked the peace pipe with them."

Will put the truck in drive and pulled away from the side of the road.

"Where are the dogs?"

"Two dogs, a box of smokes and an ounce of weed."

"I thought we weren't going to put up with any King-of-France shit?"

"It wasn't a tariff. It was a settlement. They wanted Polski."

"What did you tell them?"

"I told them Polski's crazy."

"What did they say?"

"They said they weren't afraid of crazy. Then I told them, no, he's really crazy. He's diagnosed with schizophrenia and he sees a social worker once a week."

"That was enough?"

"Most tribes respect the insane."

"Where to?" Will asked.

"Let's go the Gladstone and let Robert know everything is okay."

At the Gladstone, Will parked in the rear and they walked through the front lobby. Jimmy at the front desk said that he hadn't seen Robert all day. Will and Cobb went up to his room on the fourth floor. There was nobody there.

BARTER

COBB WALKED INTO THE small shop on Eglinton West. The smell of sandalwood incense was strong, burned to mask the strong scent of marijuana. There were shelves of records and videotapes. Bob Marley was playing in the shop. A black girl was walking around, putting things into their place. A beaded curtain hung behind the cash register. Cobb slipped through it. Philmore was asleep in a leather recliner. Cobb sat on the seat beside his and waited for him to wake. It was dangerous to wake a voodoo priest. That was when the spirits spoke to them. Cobb didn't like spirits around him. He'd had an exorcism when he was seventeen because his sleep had been so invaded by spirits. The elder had told him to control his anger, that anger draws spirits to a person and weakens them, that anger is a call to anger, and that angry things return the call, both in life and dreams. Cobb knew these things to be true. Crow was another matter altogether. Philmore had made his own deal with the spirits. Cobb could give him the simple dignity of his sleep, his communion with the spirits. After about ten minutes he woke.

He said, "Een-dee-ahn man. Nice tah see yah een-dee-ahn man."

Cobb nodded and placed a plastic bag on the TV tray between the two chairs.

"Da ganja?"

"Yeah."

Philmore opened the bag and put his face into it. "Smells good, man. Me don't know how yah grow dis ganja so fine."

"My people have been growing on this soil for a long time."

"Ah, yes, da prak-teese," Philmore said. "Me got a smahll problem wit da law man now. Me caught driving without a lie-sense, man. Me got to get da lawyer, da bullshit pile up, no?"

"It never stops," Cobb said. "The law is the sickness of these people, and where there is no law they make it up. They are lost."

"Me tinks yah is a priest, een-dee-ahn man. Me tinks yah see da Great Spirit."

Cobb said nothing, but he removed an object from his jacket and placed it on the TV tray. Philmore looked down and asked what it was. Cobb told him it was a badge. Philmore asked if it was a police badge. Cobb told him it was.

"Dat be da real ting, now, een-dee-ahn man?"

"The real thing."

Cobb assured him it was authentic. When asked where he got it, he told Philmore it had just been lying on a policeman's chest with a little pin. Cobb made it sound like it was abandoned on the sidewalk.

"Me like da spirit in yah een-dee-ahn man.

Cobb told Philmore he could have it.

Philmore took out an envelope of cash and handed it to Cobb. "What about da smokes, man, da smokes sell bettah dan da ganja."

"Will is going to come by in a few days."

"Okay, een-dee-ahn man, if yah say so. Me got a sistah dat want da strong man, she be down in Parkdale, by da een-dee-ahn man. Dat sistah need da cock all da time, man. Me give her to yah, een-dee-ahn man, for da badge, man, and for da friendship, een-dee-ahn man."

Philmore wrote an address on a piece of paper and handed it to Cobb. When Cobb took the paper, Philmore cautioned him that this was no ordinary woman. She was a powerful priestess from Brazil. The magic was strong in Brazil, Philmore told Cobb. He told Cobb he was her match. Philmore shifted in his chair.

"How dah beezness, een-dee-ahn man?"

"This quarter is very strong," Cobb said.

1109897 ONTARIO INC.

WILL WAS ON HIS way home from the movie. He walked down Roncesvalles on the eastern border of High Park. Persey had met him at the cinema. She had called a few days before. She always gave good lead time when she wanted to see him. She understood a busy life. She had a busy life. They were seeing each other less and less. Their relationship had not progressed. They still occupied a kind of primal intimacy centred on his vision and her suicide attempt. She no longer spoke about graduate school or Mrs. Rabini, and he didn't speak about cigarettes or investment scheduling. They saw themselves reflected in the other. He saw the standards up to which her mother expected her to live, the non-stop worry. She saw the collapsed will of someone who couldn't take the pressure of being precocious.

There had been a change in her, he thought, not since the last time he had seen her, but in general. She was moving in a direction he couldn't quite define. Her attire was plainer every time he saw her. That night she had worn a baggy sweater and a long wool skirt. Gone were the expensive shoes she had been wearing when he met her. In their place were heavy winter boots, flat at the heel. She wore a down-filled jacket with a hood, a wool hat, scarf and gloves. It was cold, but not that cold. She looked eccentric. It was more than just the dress. She seemed to be getting more intense each time he saw her, as though she were living by some clock that was counting down on her life. When he was with her he felt the presence of death, just as he'd felt in the church with Mrs. Duncan.

There was a chill in the air, a cool wind that crept under his jacket. He kept his hands in his pockets. The streets were still alive. He and Persey had seen the first show. It was just 9 p.m. He stopped in at a coffee shop and had a coffee and a slice of carrot cake. His vision occupied him. It always did after he saw Persey. It made him feel naked somehow. It had redefined his entire perspective, but it had not come to any definition in and of itself. It was mystical to him, a communion with some intelligence that was of him but beyond him.

He thought about Persey, her sadness, her beauty in that sadness, and the kind of person he was, one who found sadness beautiful. The news was on a small television set that sat on a brace in a corner of the ceiling. The volume was low and he could not hear everything that was being said, but the way news stories were put together it was easy enough to understand. A village of several thousand that had been hacked to death by extremists. More talk of unsafe water in Ontario. Great unrest from Mecca to Jerusalem. China was working on putting a man in space. An oil company ran a tanker aground in the north. Locally, a five-year-old boy had to watch helplessly as his terrier was torn apart by a pit bull.

The human economy was a mess.

A person is defined, Will reasoned, by what he can define and, more importantly, by how he defines things. If nothing else, his vision — a stream, a bright light, a crow, a black bear, a crucifix, a stone and purple flowers — had allowed him new possibilities for experience. By not allowing itself to be defined, and yet persisting in him as a passion, the vision forced him to consider all things undefinable. As an economist and analyst, he analyzed. At a new level he observed the grander algorithms, the greater patterns of existence. If these could be interpreted, they could be evidence of God's economy, because, he concluded, if God exists, then God would have an economy, a way of exchanging goods and services with that which it created, which, by the logic of a needs-based economy — as there are no other kinds — was the need God must have had when He created humanity. This placed God on the demand side of the exchange, because, despite God's legitimate claim of patent holder on all things seen and unseen, the patent could not generate God a profit, because God was on the demand side — the one who needs — evidenced by God's need to communicate with humanity, which, to Will's sensibilities, seemed like the thing that disrupted the human economy more than anything else.

Will wondered where Robert Polski had gone. He had been stopping by the Gladstone Hotel with some regularity, but Robert was never there, and even Jimmy, the daytime guy at the front desk, never knew where he was. Will got up and left the coffee shop. The cold evening was a balm upon his mind. The simple pleasure of a biting wind was all that was necessary. It seemed to him that happiness was a near impossibility. He tried to think of all the people he knew who were happy. There were none. There were just those who seemed to find a place, a corner of reality to hold onto by ritual and routine.

The dreams of human beings are the boundaries of an economy, which means there is a profound responsibility in dreaming. If the pursuit of space endangered the earth, in terms of its ability to sustain human existence, then there would have to be a market correction before the earth was destroyed. If Will could see it, then everyone could see it. The oxygen market was a reality; he decided then to schedule meetings with Mr. Kenny and Miguel Sanchez, *abrigado y notario*. Oxygen was the way to go, and 1109897 Ontario Inc. was in a good position to commence the acquisition of real estate, real wealth, in Costa Rica.

Will walked around the corner at King Street. It was the nicest part of the walk, so close to the lake: the wind was cold and invigorating; there wasn't much traffic, and the street walkers weren't out to harass his walk home. As he headed into a particularly dark part of King Street, where there was a large gap in the lights, he started to cry, and he thought, that poor little dog and that poor little five-year-old boy.

At that precise moment Cobb came around the corner, returning from distributing smokes to the convenience stores on Roncesvalles.

He stopped in his tracks and said, "I need you to take thirty-two cartons — assorted brands — to Mr. Kim tomorrow morning. Use the big black shoulder bag, and don't take any shit about money. He pays when he gets the smokes, not when he sells them. You can't be leaving without cash anymore. We're not a fucking bank you know."

"All right," Will said.

Cobb stepped a little closer to Will, saw the water in his eyes, and said, "What the fuck is the matter with you?"

DEVIL WOMAN

COBB GLANCED DOWN AT the paper Philmore had given him. The numbers were easy to read. Philmore's handwriting was immaculate. The sign outside the address said Psychic. There was a little neon replication of a crystal ball. Cobb walked in the front door. The interior was lit well and gaudy. Horrible prints clung to the walls and the furniture was tacky and the colours all clashed, not that Cobb was any great decorator himself, but the place even smelled of disharmony, the environment seemed to come out of a disturbed mind. He sat down in one of the chairs and waited for someone to respond to the bells that had chimed when he opened the door. A couple of minutes later a fat black woman in her fifties came into the room. She smiled at Cobb and asked if he was there for a reading. He said, "No, I'm here to see Fatima."

The woman said, "Just a moment." She turned and left the room. A few minutes later Fatima entered. She had on a blouse that revealed her ample cleavage. Her hair was black and curly, thick and wild. She wore a cotton skirt and black leather pumps. She had beautiful thick lips and a beautiful copper face, but her eyes were most striking. Her eyes were coal black. There was no distinction between iris and pupil.

It was impossible to guess her reaction to being called by name to the waiting room. He could not tell if she had been expecting him or was surprised to see him. He could not tell if she was afraid, curious, contemptuous or irritated. She walked to his chair and crouched down beside him. He smelled lavender. Her hair brushed up against his arm. It was soft.

She said, "You are here to see me."

"I am."

She took his hand and led him down a flight of stairs at the back of the building. They descended into darkness. She let go and left him for a moment. A light turned on and he looked around. It was an old cellar. The three-storey building was probably close to one hundred years old. It smelled like a cellar, but he only recognized the smell when the light went on. There were whips, a cross with leather straps, and other things he didn't recognize. There were a lot of candles and tall mirrors and there was a red circle crudely drawn on the cellar floor.

"You have come for the punishment," she said.

"No."

She showed her first sign of emotion, puzzlement, he guessed.

"Then what?" she asked.

"Philmore sent me," he said.

"Philmore," she said, walked over and circled him, touching him lightly on different parts of his body with her fingertips. He tingled.

"You are a man then?" she asked.

"I am a man," he said.

"We will see," she said, took him by the hand and led him back up the stairs, back down the hall, up another flight of stairs and into a room. It had a small lamp covered with a thin red sash that coloured the light a soft red. There was a bed and nothing else.

"Take your clothes off," she said.

He began to disrobe and she left the room. He placed his clothes in a corner and stood naked in the room with his hands behind his back. There was a small window covered with black curtains. It was very quiet and he had to struggle to hear the street noises. The door opened again and Fatima entered with a chicken in a cage and a small tape player. She told him to lie on his back on the bed. He did what he was told, not because he followed orders, but because that was what he wanted to do. She looked into his face and her black eyes were hypnotic. She turned on the tape recorder and drum music filled the room. It added to the power of her gaze. She took off her clothes slowly and sensually, never releasing him from her eyes. When she was naked she took the chicken from the cage and slit its throat with a knife. A good knife, Cobb noted. The chicken screamed and wriggled. There was blood all over her and all over the floor. The chicken collapsed after a few minutes. The drum music continued. Fatima's eyes were still on him. With blood on her breasts and abdomen she climbed onto the bed and onto his hard cock. Her sex was powerful. She rode him relentlessly. It was like she was channelling something through her. She was sharing her ecstasy with a host of unseen things. When she finished, she fell off him and was unconscious before she hit the bed. He wasn't given a chance to cum. He got onto his knees and jerked himself off onto her bloodied breasts. She didn't wake up. He got off the bed. He put his clothes on over the blood because there was nothing to wash himself with and he didn't want to go looking for a bathroom. As he laced up his boots, he saw the dead chicken. He looked to the bed. Fatima was still asleep. He stood and stared at the chicken for a moment. He snatched up its headless, bloody form.

No sense in letting it go to waste, he thought.

On the way out he crossed paths with a black cat.

BLACK MALE

IN HIS DREAM THERE was nobody on the street, but this didn't strike PC Richard Chase as odd. The street lights were on. He looked at his wristwatch. It was blank. There was a white light over its surface. He looked down at his chest and his badge was there. It felt good on his chest. He felt a pulse between his legs. His cock was half full of blood. It felt good to be a cop.

There was an itch on his chest where his badge was. He scratched it without looking down. It persisted. He looked down again and there was a spider coming out of his badge. He slammed on the brakes, jumped out of the car and pulled the badge off his chest. He threw it to the ground and the spider ran away. A spider came out of my badge, he thought. A spider came out of my badge. Before he could think about that any further the silence hit him. There wasn't a sound in the city. The whole of Parkdale was quiet: there was no traffic, no people, no electrical hum. He could hear his breathing, heavy and deep because of the adrenaline jolt the spider had caused him. Why was it so quiet? The radio in the car was working. He heard his division sergeant's voice on the radio. He heard other officers on the radio, but where were they? He had to call somebody. Something had happened to all the energy in Parkdale. He got out of the cruiser and walked around. The entire community had disappeared. He walked back to the car and tried to open the door. It was locked. I'm locked out of my cruiser, he thought, another embarrassment as a cop. He had his portable radio, the one attached to his belt, but that was a last resort. There was no way he was going to call the division and ask for a patrol car to come by with another set of keys to his cruiser.

He started to walk down the quiet and empty street. It was like being a beat cop. He had done that for a couple of years. His penis started to get hard again. It felt good to be a cop. What a strange and wonderful place, he thought. He knew of a donut shop just up the street, so he thought that he would walk there, get a coffee and call a tow truck from the pay phone. The tow-truck drivers all carried the tools to unlock his door.

As he approached the donut shop he saw it was empty. The lights were on. The coffee was on the burner and slight wisps of steam were coming from the tops of the two coffee pots. He pulled to open the door. It was locked. There was no Back in Five Minutes sign. He sat down on the curb. He hoped that the proprietor would come out of the bathroom, that the proprietor would know what was going on, why there was nobody on the streets, no traffic, no noise.

Three people came into view. They came out from under the railway bridge and walked toward the donut shop. As they got closer he noticed that they were black, male, and between eighteen and twenty-five, a high-crime demographic, if the Metro Toronto Police profiled by crime statistics. He stood up. They approached.

"What are you doing, cop?" the tallest said.

"What?"

"I ask the questions here."

Chase reached for the handset to his belt radio.

"Officer in need of assistance, corner of Queen and Dufferin."

"Situation," a voice said back on the radio.

"I've got three black males coming at me."

"Fuck you, cracker," another of the black males said.

Chase pulled his revolver, unlatched the safety and squeezed the trigger without any warning or any order to the three black males. There was no boom, no recoil, nothing. There were no bullets in his gun. His heart started to beat crazy fast. His mind raced. He turned and started to run. He could hear their footsteps behind him. He could hear their laughter. He looked down beside him, at the cracked sidewalk rushing past under his full sprint. He saw his badge with eight hairy legs on it, running beside him, pacing him.

Dr. Bluette made notes on the dream. Dick Chase was recounting the same dream over and over again. Well, in fairness, she wrote, the details were not a one-to-one correlation. The expressions of fear, guilt and racial paranoia were significantly different in each of the dreams. It wasn't her place to tell him that he was probably intimidated by his belief in the myth of the black man's penis size. Most violence derives from the sexual impulse. In these dreams the recurring detail was the spider, and here was where Dr. Bluette earned her bread. She had to nail this down. Chase had come to her with a general impotence of character, a cop who had been assaulted on the streets of Parkdale, then further reduced by the theft of his badge and bullets. But he had not come with bad dreams. She believed that the spider was the dream manifestation of his fear of change. The spider he described had fur on its legs, which implied molting, and what is molting but the process of rebirth, redefinition, the resurrection of the psyche. Pragmatism made her write *psychotic side effects* in her Zolfax journal.

Cobb listened to the audio tape from the session.

Dr. Bluette concluded their session on that point.

Cobb put the material back in the cabinet. He didn't have much free time anymore. Business was booming. He maintained an interest in Chase's therapy because he had created the need for it. He had just dropped by to break into his doctor's office and catch up with the wounded constable's sessions. Now he had to go meet some Mohawks and renegotiate prices based on the new economy of scale Will had created.

CHICKEN

COBB WALKED DOWN THE street with his black bag. It had been two weeks since his first and only encounter with Fatima. He had no phone number, only her address. He shouldn't feel strange about not calling her for two weeks, or not dropping by the day after they met, killed a chicken and copulated. He was acutely aware of the new territory his sex encompassed; it frightened him. The Gladstone had served him well. New territory meant new risk. Cobb was always aware of his shadow in the world. He had to guard himself. He lived in shadows. Taking any woman outside of the hotel made a shadow. Many things hunted by shadows alone, Cobb included. It was not good to make a shadow. The Brazilian witch was powerful.

The contents of his black bag made Cobb feel awkward. Fatima was the first woman he was visiting since his release from Warkworth. He was bringing an offering, not a gift. He was obliged to make an offering. She had spilled blood on their first meeting.

He entered the building. The same black woman was there. When she saw Cobb, she turned right around and went up the stairs. Moments later Fatima appeared. She looked as good as she had the first time he saw her. She pointed to the sofa and he sat down. She sat down beside him and pointed her knees in his direction.

"Your name," she said.

"Cobb."

"The chicken?" she asked.

"I ate it," he answered.

"You are very brave," she said. She smiled and she looked beautiful to Cobb when she was happy. "You cleaned it first?" she asked.

"I'm not a savage," he answered. "I plucked the feathers, gutted it, cooked it and ate it."

"It was good?"

"Nothing like fresh meat."

"Yes," she said. She reached over, took his hand and walked him upstairs.

He didn't have to be told what to do this time. He undressed and got on the bed. She came in a moment later with the tape player, and turned the drum music on.

"No chicken?" he asked.

"Only the first time," she answered, "to make sure you are clean."

Cobb nodded his head. It wasn't complicated.

She pulled something out of her skirt and brought it up to her nose. Cobb couldn't see what it was, her hands were covering it. She inhaled through her nostrils, one at a time, fell back a step, dizzy and disoriented, then she snapped back into position in front of the bed, her eyes crazy and wild. She jumped on him again and rode him until she was sated, then fell off, unconscious, the way she had the first time.

Cobb did the same thing he had done the last time — he jerked himself off on her breasts; but, instead of leaving this time, he waited for her to wake. She slept for about thirty minutes then roused herself into wakefulness.

"Where did you go?" he asked.

"This I can not speak about," she said.

"Is it okay that I stayed?" he asked.

"Yes," she said. "It is."

Cobb dressed and she dressed. They went downstairs to the kitchen and she made tea. They didn't speak. The black woman was not to be seen. Cobb unzipped the black bag and pulled his out his offering.

She looked at the chicken on her kitchen table.

"I wouldn't want you to think I was freeloading," Cobb said.

"It's very sweet," she said.

Cobb said, "So what's this punishment thing in your basement?"

"The dungeon? Oh, it's very good money," she said. "I need a partner for the girl-men."

"Girl-men?"

"The fags. You mind the fags?"

"Not at all."

"Good," she said. "I teach you. Next week I have to go north. You feed my cat? I can give you a key."

"What about the other woman who lives here?"

"She is my employee. I can't ask her to feed the cat."

"Okay."

"Good."

Cobb left Fatima's house and walked home. He was plagued by the thought, Do I have a girlfriend now?

BRIGHT LIGHT

COBB AND WILL WALKED down the street. It was nearly three in the morning. They were going home after another night at Fatima's. They were learning the slave trade. It was $300 per hour. Three slaves a week was another four thousand a month. It was a worthwhile sideline, Will thought, so long as Cobb was able to do it, and who knew, Will pointed out, somewhere down the line they could get a webcam and maybe host a site. E-commerce was a new market that 1109897 Ontario Inc. could finance through a development phase and, even if it flopped, the write-off would be of value. They had to think strategically. The emergence of the slave market was fortuitous for 1109897 Ontario Inc. Cobb had no problem with any of it. He wore a mask the whole time.

A lot of the slaves liked to visit in the wee hours of the night. It was none of Cobb's and Will's concern. So long as they had the money, any time was fine. Will noticed that Cobb did not need his sleep. He got up every day and went to work. He never seemed tired. He slept only a couple of hours a night, sometimes not at all.

It was bitterly cold and getting colder. It was thirty below. Will had not dressed properly. He was shivering, in danger of biting his lower lip. He had his arms inside his jacket, wrapped around his body, his hands moving up and down along his ribs, the arms of his jacket flapping in the wind. Cobb was unaffected by the cold. His massive body seemed like it had its own sun somewhere in his belly that sent all the heat he needed out to his extremities. He walked with his hands at his sides, no gloves. His jacket wasn't even zipped up.

They passed by an alleyway and Cobb's peripheral vision caught a lump of something that was not garbage or refuse or anything else that could be dismissed. He turned and darted into the alley. It was a sleeping bag. There was form in it. Cobb touched the bag. There was no response. Cobb touched the bag again, this time pushing into it. He felt something hard. He pulled back the sleeping bag and there was a body. It was cold and hard and without any of the colour that spoke of life.

"Fuck."

Will pulled in behind him. He peered past Cobb's crouched form. He saw the face.

"Oh, shit."

"It's Polski," Cobb said.

"Oh, shit," Will said. "I haven't seen him since he knocked out that prospect. He just disappeared." Will started to shiver uncontrollably, all of his warmth had been grabbed by Robert Polski's invisible hand as he was being dragged away to some other place.

Cobb said, "He was a good man."

"He liked to talk about prophets."

"Poor bastard."

"What do we do? Call the police?"

"No police," Cobb said.

"What is he doing out here?"

"He didn't like sleeping indoors."

"Let's get out of here," Will said.

"No." Cobb picked up Robert and tucked him under his arm. He walked out of the alley carrying the frozen man like a large lunch box.

"What are you going to do?" Will asked.

"Follow me."

Cobb headed off. He was actually quicker with Polski under his arm than he had been without the added weight. The sleeping bag fell off Robert's head a couple of times and Will saw the frozen eyes, closed, and the hair knotted and dirty and frozen into clumps. Cobb steered them back to Mrs. Duncan's rooming house. He gently stashed the body beside the house, out of sight, and told Will to go in quietly and put on some warmer clothes. Will unlocked the door and crept up the stairs. He put two sweaters on, an extra pair of socks. He grabbed a wool hat and a pair of leather gloves. He crept back down the stairs, out the door, gently closing it behind him. Cobb got up off the front step where he had been sitting and waiting. He picked Polski up again and started to walk south, toward the lake. They covered much the same path that Will used to take every morning in the summer, when he walked to the lake for solitude and reflection, except, instead of going to the lake, instead of crossing the pedestrian path over the expressway, Cobb turned east, toward the downtown.

There was a vast expanse of undeveloped land that Will had not seen before. Built from scrap wood, there were small huts and other makeshift lodgings. It was a meagre community of homeless people, asleep, except for a few around low fires in steel drums, warming their hands, drinking wine and talking. Cobb and Will moved through them in silence. They saw Cobb. They saw Will. They saw the body under Cobb's arm. Some left their fires and disappeared into their huts. Cobb walked farther along, past the living space, then gently placed Polski down.

"Gather scrap wood, but not anything these people might build with," Cobb said to Will, and Will did as he was told.

In five minutes they had a large pile of scrap wood, newspaper, bits of insulation, and other things that would burn. Cobb took the sleeping bag off Robert. He then stripped Robert of his long coat, his shirt, his pants, his undergarments, and his shoes and socks. He threw these things into a pile away from the pyre. He arranged the now naked man beside the flammables and lit the newspaper. A dim flame appeared. It spread quickly. Soon the wood was lapped by flame. It was orange and yellow, and then a little bit blue as some of the chemicals in the insulation burned.

Cobb wanted to wait until there were some good coals before putting Polski's body on the fire. Will stood to the side, in near disbelief, wanting to believe Cobb wasn't really going to burn Robert, and then thinking, What's wrong with burning him? That's what the city would do. That or bury him in some pauper graveyard. At least this way two people who knew him would be beside him when he went through his final transformation.

From a distance they saw a bright light. Because it came from nowhere and there were no roads, it was a curious thing to both of them. It was a single light, therefore not a car. As it got closer, Will became aware of just how bright it was. Its first appearance must have been from several kilometres away, because it was slow in approaching them, slow in its growing luminosity. Cobb crouched down and put a hand to the cold and frozen earth. "Train," he said.

Will looked down and noticed that just beyond the fire were train tracks.

"Passenger?" Will asked.

"No, this is a freight line," Cobb said.

The light continued to approach. It carved itself out of the darkness. In a few minutes they heard the engine and then it was upon them, an incredibly bright light, which was actually two, one atop the other, in the centre of the engine. The train roared past and the earth quaked under their feet, a long string of cars following behind. It took more than ten minutes to pass. Will and Cobb stood transfixed by its thunderous, earth-shaking presence.

When the train had passed, and the night and silence had returned, they turned back to their business. Polski was sitting up beside the fire, in the snow, completely naked.

"It's a miracle," Will said.

LAZARUS

"IT WAS REALLY REMARKABLE," Robert said. He sat across from Will in a booth at the Dolphin. "I died. I can't remember everything. I just remember this tremendous sense of belonging, on a scale that I have never even considered before. I only consider it now because I remember that feeling of belonging. I can't forget it."

"But did you see anything?" Will asked. "Were there any visions?"

"I started to see things just before I woke up beside the fire. They were like dreams, but they weren't dreams. They had so much energy, so much knowledge. It was like each one was a single sentence spoken by some giant intelligence, and it revealed a scope of knowledge that I accepted, like I had always known it but forgotten...."

"Yes," Will said.

"— and there was just so much beauty and acceptance and belonging in that knowledge, but even it was a lesser sense of belonging than the place I was coming back from. Then the world started to speak, and I started to mix the dreams with the world, so the awareness of the fire on my body became fire in my dream. The sound of the train became thunder. The dream went dark and then exploded with thunderous light. Then I woke up."

"That's amazing," Will said.

Robert leaned back.

"You're like Lazarus," Will said.

Cobb walked into the Dolphin and up to the booth where Will and Robert sat.

"You have a lot of nerve quitting smoking," Cobb said to Robert.

Dorothy came up behind Cobb and tapped him on the shoulder. She opened her mouth to speak, but Cobb cut her off. He pointed to Robert and said, "I brought this bum back to life and he repays me by quitting smoking."

"Unh-huh," Dorothy said, and then she tugged at his arm and leaned into his ear, "Fred says the RCMP was in here asking about cigarettes."

"That fucking black cat," Cobb said.

BLACKOUT

WILL WAS EXTREMELY MOVED by the resurrection of Robert Polski. He took it as a sign. Why wouldn't he? He had been following a vision for three seasons. He likened himself to those monks who set out looking for the next incarnation of the Dalai Lama. They followed a series of signs to the newborn spiritual leader. When they found him, they had a number of tests for him. Of course, Polski was only the incarnation of himself, brought back to life after being frozen and then heated up like packaged food in a microwave.

It was the kind of cold where Will could see his breath just as if he were smoking. He made it to the donut shop in under fifteen minutes. Persey was late. She had called him that day. She wanted to meet. She sounded ecstatic. He was curious, and cautious. Sudden mood swings were not a good sign in someone with scars on her wrists. He was halfway through his coffee when Persey showed up. Will noticed when she sat down that her belly was big enough to give away that she was pregnant. She clothed herself in loose dresses and thick sweaters. She still hadn't told her mother.

She couldn't keep the secret much longer, and the stress of the whole situation was real. She got a coffee, sat down and said, "You're never going to believe what happened to me this week." She launched into her story.

She had been to the hospital four times in the last six days. She had developed an attachment to Mrs. Rabini. She couldn't help herself. She had voiced her objections to shock treatment, citing Mrs. Rabini's age, but the doctors had paid her no attention. "We can't get too attached. This is what's best for the patient," Dr. Singh had said. If Persey was intent on fulfilling the one-year mandate she had set for herself with Mrs. Rabini, it would be best for her to observe and draw conclusions on the value of electric shock therapy. Persey had wanted to extend her work into the Rabini family. She had wanted to document the emotional affects on Mrs. Rabini and her husband, who had looked terribly distraught the times Persey had seen him at the hospital. He and his wife would sit at one of the tables in the cafeteria and cut salami and cheese, eat together and say very little. His face was afflicted with sadness and helplessness.

Persey had observed Mrs. Rabini's shock therapy with a muted disgust. Afterward, she threw up in the staff washroom. She assured Will it had nothing to do with the pregnancy. That same day, Persey had placed the car in reverse to pull out of the hospital parking lot, when she noticed the grounds surrounding the hospital were one of the most pleasant and undisturbed areas of Parkdale. It was like an Indian burial ground, she said to Will. The streets were busy and traffic was stop-and-start on Queen Street West. She'd felt an anxiety attack coming over her. She'd been fighting with these anxiety attacks for weeks. It can't be good for the baby, she told Will. Most times she would feel a tremendous angst in her gut, then she would start to feel a tingling in her head, like she was going to lose consciousness, but that hadn't happened. When the light turned green she had mustered all of her resolve and strength, put her foot to the peddle, and started to move through the intersection, when suddenly everything went out: the street lights, traffic lights, store lights, everything. Total darkness.

She was referring to the twenty-minute blackout West Toronto had experienced the previous day. On the news they were trying to calm people, insisting it wasn't an energy shortage in one of the coldest winters on record, but, rather, a freak accident. Nobody mentioned terrorists, though it passed through everybody's mind.

Persey continued with her story. She had passed out behind the wheel of her mother's Land Rover. When her eyes opened, there was a man in the passenger seat of her car. The window had been broken and the door was still open, letting in the biting cold.

The man had said, "Don't worry. I'm a cop. My name is Chase. You passed out."

She looked at Will, shook her head and sipped her coffee. The thing that struck her the most was what she called the "weird symmetry" between shocking Mrs. Rabini and the power around the hospital going out right at the end of her shift. Will agreed that it was an odd thing. But there was a greater coincidence, she told Will. The man who came to her rescue was a patient of her mother's. That struck Will as quite odd indeed. Her mother was surprised to learn from Persey that she had met Richard Chase and that he had commented on Persey's last name being the same as his shrink.

"What a story," Will said.

"Isn't it, though? I mean what are the chances?"

"It's like a waking dream," Will said.

"And so we're going to go out ... me and the cop."

"Oh?" Will said.

Will knew what had caused the blackout. He'd caught Cobb making a bomb from gunpowder he extracted from bullets. He had put the bomb together in the second floor kitchen of Mrs. Duncan's rooming house. Will had tried to talk him out of his decision to go into the sewers to disrupt the electrical service in the neighbourhood, but Cobb had made up his mind. Several blocks from where Persey had passed out, and probably only a few minutes after her blackout, a manhole cover had slid aside and a pumpkin-sized head popped out and looked from side to side for a quick reconnaissance. The street was empty and black. Cobb had popped out of the hole with a flashlight and a tool box in his hands. He walked swiftly but casually to where Will, his lookout, had waited with a cellphone.

BLACK BEAR

Cobb was a natural with "the punishment," as Fatima called it. He worked through Fatima, her dungeon, her network of contacts, her knowledge of the trade and its practice. He franchised her punishment business and took it into another market, and like a good franchisee, he paid residuals to the franchiser. A session was $350. Fatima kept $50 for every session. Cobb also set her up in the marijuana businesses. She could move a pound a week in quarter bags. She mentioned that many of her clients asked for ecstasy, but Cobb refused to find a supplier, saying simply, "Street chemicals are bad medicine." But, aside from that one restriction, Fatima's dungeon was one-stop shopping for the depraved.

It didn't matter to Cobb that he had to dress up in black leather and flog middle-aged white men. He could hardly believe he was getting paid to do it. Will went with Cobb. He watched a small black and white television in the kitchen, and he answered the phone and the door. Cobb needed moral support for the punishment business. He was seeing eight to twelve slaves a week and putting all the money into 1109897 Ontario Inc. It was as lucrative as the sale of cigarettes, but it was a change — and still good money, by any account. The least Will could do was handle the schedule. It would be an awkward situation to double book the dungeon. The last thing one slave wanted was to meet another. Fatima had been very careful to explain this to them.

Most of the men just wanted to be humiliated by another man. They weren't even gay. They weren't straight either. They were something else, something people didn't like to give names to and something people didn't like to talk about a whole lot, which made it a great business from the practitioner's position. Although Cobb could find no laws in the Criminal Code of Canada against it, it could always be interpreted by the peacekeepers or whatever powers that be as something unsavory. The law had a way of finding its victims the way that a poison gas slips under doors. No matter how well a person thought they were sheltered, there was always a possibility they could be charged with something.

The slaves were stupid, Cobb realized in short time. Some fear taxed their spirit, and they felt the need to purify, which was completely natural to Cobb, but the slaves made no progress. Cobb had no mercy for their stupidity. He took their money.

One of the routines that Cobb had worked up for the slaves was the bear routine. In the bear routine, Cobb would appear in the dungeon, after the slave had been prepared, which meant being told what to do by Will or Fatima, who met the slaves at the door and walked them down to the dungeon, instructed them to undress, blindfold themselves and wait on their hands and knees for the master. Cobb was given no name. He was just referenced as "the master." Will or Fatima would walk up to the second floor and tell Cobb that there was a slave ready in the dungeon. It was the only way he could do it. If they never saw his face it was bearable. Fatima had started him out in a simple leather mask. If he wanted to tell the slave to take his blindfold off, he could do so in the assurance that he would not be seen. The bear routine had Cobb in the dungeon in the skin of a black bear, the bear head perfectly cleaned and preserved with dark glass eyes. It scared the hell out of the poor bastards and it gave Cobb a good kick. He rarely spoke to the slaves. His voice could not be heard well through the bear skin and he had a little difficulty seeing because he had to peer out the open and snarling mouth of the bear, so he gestured to the slaves, lifting his arm up under a bear arm and pointing at some piece of equipment in the dungeon. Cobb could conduct a one-hour session in almost total silence. Some of the slaves liked to ask questions. That pissed Cobb off. Sometimes he would give them a kick in the ass, but he had to be careful, as Fatima constantly reminded him: this was fantasy.

On this particular night at Fatima's house, a month into the operation, a slave came by. Will greeted him at the door politely, took his jacket, hung it up in the closet and guided the man down to the dungeon. He gave the usual directions and told the man the master would be down in a moment. He went up the stairs where Cobb was watching an episode of *Cheers* on the small black and white television in the kitchen, the volume turned low so as not to disturb Fatima, who had gone to bed. Sam Malone was making time with some tart in the bar, and Diane had a problem with the shallowness of it. Cobb liked Sam Malone. Will sat and watched a few minutes of the show. It was better to let the slaves wait in the near darkness of the basement for a while. It put them in the right mind.

Cobb stood and put on the bear skin. Will started to laugh. He always laughed when Cobb was dressed in costume. Cobb was not beyond providing amusement, growling or snarling once the head had slipped over his and it was impossible to recognize him. He descended to the basement. He walked into the dungeon and stood immobile. The slave looked up and Cobb said nothing. The slave said, "I like to be a bad boy."

Cobb thought he was in a stupid sitcom himself. He sat down on the one chair in the dungeon and faced the slave with the bear skin concealing him. The slave became confused and embarrassed.

The slave said, "What do you want me to do?"

Cobb flipped the bear skin off, looked square at the man and said, "You can do whatever you want, Alexander, but there's no fucking way you're getting your three-fifty back."

Alexander Campbell, QC, bolted up and grabbed his clothes. He ran up the stairs, grabbed his wool overcoat off the coat rack, and ran naked out the front door and into the frigid early morning darkness.

Cobb climbed the stairs to watch the end of the *Cheers* episode. Alexander Campbell, QC, was the only slave scheduled for that night. He and Will could go home any time.

GRIM TALE

WILL WAS INVITED TO the Bluette home on the Saturday of Easter weekend. The home was stunning. It was located in Toronto's downtown. It had passed through four generations of Bluettes, beginning with Persey's maternal great-grandmother. Persey knew that the home was her birthright and that she would continue the family tradition. Persey gave Will the tour. There were fourteen rooms. She showed him where her mother slept as a child, and her grandmother. She showed him the box behind the furnace, full of dolls from four generations of Bluette girls. There had not been more than one child for each generation of the last four generations. Persey told him all this standing beside the furnace, under a bare sixty-watt bulb.

"That's kind of odd," Will said.

"Mental health is the newest mutation," Persey said. "When you're raised in an experiment you want to conduct them for the rest of your life."

She turned off the light and they went back up the creaky wooden steps. Persey's mother could be heard in the kitchen. She sensed their proximity and called, "Red wine?"

"Please, Mother."

Will leaned in close to Persey's ear as they walked into the kitchen. "I don't drink," he said.

"You do tonight," she said back and she caught his eyes to underscore the importance of what she had said. "Mother abhors abstainers," she whispered.

"Ah, there you are," Dr. Irene Bluette said as she spun around.

Dr. Bluette wore a pair of faded blue jeans and a wool sweater. She looked cool to Will, like a young person in an older person's body. She was attractive. A lot of care went into her hair, her face, her nails and her body. She took care of herslf. Will had seen the treadmill and weights in the basement. He remembered his first meeting with Persey, her facade, the brave face on a crumbling interior.

Persey and her mother lived well, Will noted. No complaint could be made for comfort. The dining room table was antique walnut. The end tables in the sitting room were gorgeous. Most of the furniture was part of the house's history, part of its dowry. The art work was all original Group of Seven and David Milne. The renovations on the house probably cost more than most people spent on their first homes. Dr. Bluette must have a good accountant, Will thought.

"Here you each are," she said, her hands outstretched with two glasses of wine. Will and Persey took their wine. Persey's mother had informed them that dinner would be a few more minutes and that they should use the time to get better acquainted. They all sat down in the living room.

"Now, William. Is it William or Bill or ...?"

"Will," Persey said. "He goes by Will, Mother."

"Will it is then. Now, Will, what is this little bit of intelligence Persey has brought to me? You're working on a new economic system?"

"No. Nothing like that," Will said. "I just talk about economics a lot because it's the only thing I really know anything about."

"I see," Dr. Bluette said. She reached over and opened the drawer to a small end table beside her armchair. She pulled out a joint and lit it.

"Oh, Christ, Mother," Persey said.

"What?" Dr. Bluette responded. "It's practically legal."

Responding to a timer on the stove, Dr. Bluette said, "Dinner will be served in three minutes." Awkwardly, Persey got up and marched into the kitchen. It seemed to Will that Dr. Bluette had yet to notice her daughter's advancing pregnancy. She did not offer to help Persey in the kitchen. Instead, she passed the joint to Will. He had never smoked marijuana but, with Persey in the kitchen and no direction, he fell to the first rule, which was: Do what mother does. He took the joint and inhaled deeply. He coughed violently and gulped down his wine when his breath returned to him. His throat felt dry and parched. Dr. Bluette promptly filled his wine glass. She nodded and pointed to the joint. "Again," she said. And so he did. He took another deep haul off the joint. Coughed again. Gulped down his second glass of wine when his breath returned. Dr. Bluette filled his glass a third time. She stood and went into the kitchen. Persey returned. He saw her standing over him as a kind of mirage. He couldn't quite get a bead on her. Her face came close to his and he heard her whisper in his ear, "Be careful. She's dangerous."

"What?" Will said.

"Mother's like a Grimm's Fairly Tale." Persey took his hand and helped him stand up. Once standing he took a deep breath and everything came into focus. They walked into the dining room. The table had a beautiful glazed ham on it, mashed potatoes, corn, fresh rolls, butter and two bottles of red wine.

"Grace?" Dr. Bluette said. She looked at Will.

"I've never known it," Will said.

"No," Dr. Bluette said. "Grace. Would you please say grace?"

"Oh," Will said. He took the stoned doctor's outstretched hand into his own as a symbol of love and trust, and he took Persey's outstretched hand as well, and into the circle of love and fellowship they formed he said, "Thank you, God, for this meal and for this moment." He released their hands.

They ate their dinner and made small talk. Dr. Bluette inquired about Persey's matriculation, her professors, her thesis advisor, her timeline and Mrs. Rabini. Persey was still traumatized by the shock therapy applied to the old woman. Her mother was trying to convince her that that there was nothing to be traumatized by, that the shock therapy had been decided upon and executed by professionals. Persey's immature attachment was pointless, uninformed and self-indulgent.

Will felt underwater. He found it difficult to draw anything into focus. He heard the noises made by the silverware scraping the plates and the voices of Persey and her mother like bright fish swimming past him. He found it difficult to make sense of anything. He ate a second helping of potatoes and ham. It levelled him off a bit.

"Don't you agree, Will?" Dr. Bluette asked.

"About the electric shock therapy?" he said.

"Yes," Dr. Bluette said.

"I don't know," Will said. "I've never shocked anybody."

"Well, then just as a mental health practitioner, do you think Persey should be emotionally involved with a patient?"

"It's her first?" Will asked.

"Yes," Persey interjected, overjoyed by Will's possible support.

"If she doesn't feel empathy for what the patient feels, how is she ever going to be a good doctor?"

Dr. Bluette moved her head in a manner suggestive of thought, her eyes cast up to the ceiling of the dining room.

"That's a point of consideration," she said.

They were pretty much finished with the main course. Dr. Bluette and Persey cleared the table and brought out coffee and digestive biscuits, which they ate right from the Peek Frean package. The half-smoked joint was in an ashtray Dr. Bluette had placed on the dining room table. Dr. Bluette lit it and sipped her coffee. She passed it to Will. He took another haul.

"You smoke marijuana?" Persey said.

"No," Will answered and he took another haul before passing the joint back to Dr. Bluette.

Persey looked at her mother. "Mother, Will's not used...."

"Oh, Jesus, he'll be fine," Dr. Bluette said. "It's just weed."

Dr. Bluette looked at Will and smiled. He smiled back.

"Do you practise any faith, Will?" she asked.

"Pardon?"

"It's Easter. Do you practise any faith?"

"Ah, the resurrection," Will said. "Powerful story." His head tilted a little.

"I take it you're a believer?" Dr. Bluette said.

"Believe? What's to believe?" Will said. "I resurrected a guy in the middle of February."

Dr. Bluette filled their wine glasses again.

"I see. So what do you do, Will?" Dr. Bluette asked.

"What do you mean?" Will asked.

"I mean day-to-day. How do you live? Do you work?"

"I started a small import and export business with a partner. There's a pretty good return from it, so I'm all right for rent and stuff, and it keeps me pretty well occupied. I don't have any complaints."

"Where do you import from?" Dr. Bluette asked.

"Ontario," Will said.

Dr. Bluette looked puzzled for a moment. "Well, that's not really importing, is it?" she asked. "There aren't any foreign regulations. It isn't even interprovincial trade."

"I guess."

"Persey told me you had a degree in economics?"

"I do."

"Would it be a commodity then?" Dr. Bluette laughed. "My God, you're not a fur trader are you?"

"No furs," Will said.

"Well, what then?"

"Mother," Persey said.

"I'm not allowed to ask?"

"It's fine," Will said.

"I'm buying the future of our species. I'm buying oxygen from the rain forest."

"How do you buy oxygen?" Dr. Bluette asked.

"You don't," Will said. "You buy land that produces oxygen and sell carbon bonds."

"That's got to be the most cynical thing I've ever heard," Dr. Bluette said.

"Running electricity through people's brains is cynical. I'm a realist, like Linus. You're a dreamer, like Charlie Brown."

Dr. Bluette looked at Persey. People usually didn't speak to her in this manner, but Will was drunk and stoned.

"I have some work to do," Dr. Bluette said as she started to get up from the table.

"Christ was kind of a flake, don't you think?" Will said.

"Excuse me?" Dr. Bluette said.

"Well, come on, I mean, this Son of God thing, that's a little extreme, don't you think?"

"What do you mean?" Dr. Bluette leaned into the table. Her eyes were intense.

"Why would the Son of God speak to a bunch of sheep herders and fishermen in the Middle East?"

"Will?" Persey said.

"I've just sort of come to the conclusion that He was a flake."

"A flake?" Dr. Bluette said.

"Yes, a flake," Will said. "I mean, his intentions were good. The love stuff is good and true and He's one of the most decent human beings I've ever read about, but the marketing is all wrong. I think the whole thing, the entire Christian thing went wrong with that one phrase, 'Son of God.' I mean, what must it be like to be a Jew, a Muslim, a Taoist or whatever else and come into contact with this idea of a biological progeny of God? It's ludicrous and, for that matter, if He knew everything, then why didn't He know that his actions would cause way more harm than good, all the wars, the deaths, the carnage. He's responsible for a lot of it."

"Young man," Dr. Bluette said, but she was cut off by Will, who was caught up in his moment.

"And if He knew his actions would lead to his death, then He was suicidal, right? How would you diagnose him? Would you shock him, too?"

Dr. Bluette turned red in the face.

"It was his mission," she screamed.

Will let his head fall softly to the table. He closed his eyes.

Persey started to cry.

"What's the matter, honey?" Dr. Bluette asked.

She sobbed and said, "I'm pregnant."

"I didn't do it," Will said, his head popping up for a moment with his eyes still shut.

"Oh, for Christ's sake! " Dr. Bluette said.

That was the last thing Will remembered before passing out. When he awoke fifteen minutes later, Persey and her mother were above him. He was lying on the dining room floor. Dr. Bluette was prepping a needle. Will turned his head to the side and vomited on the Persian rug.

"Where's the bathroom?" he said.

Persey helped him up and took him to the main floor powder room. He emptied his stomach into the toilet. He came out of the powder room a few minutes later and he was alone. He could hear Persey and her mother talking down the hall. He slipped his boots and jacket on and left through the side door. When he got outside he was completely disoriented. He turned the wrong way and ended up stomping through the snow and slush in the backyard. Persey saw him first.

"Oh my God," she said. "He's going into the woods."

Dr. Bluette ran to the front of the house, put on her boots and winter jacket and took off after Will.

He lost his footing and rolled partway down the side of the ravine. The snow was deep in some parts, and Will sank in up to his waist, but he managed to get through it and took refuge at the base of a large oak tree. There was a full moon and the barren branches of the trees sang a soft sound. The wind pushed through the ravine. His breathing was heavy. He heard his name in the wind and it chilled him to his bones. He thought he had gone completely mad until he saw the figure of Dr. Bluette coming down the side of the ravine, sinking in the deep snow as he had, a parka, the hood pulled up and tightened around her face.

"Wiiiiilllllliam!" she called.

He got up and tried to run. He had the simple and childlike fear of a Grimm's Fairy Tale in him. He tried to run. He stopped only a couple of times to dry heave. It took more than an hour for him to find a road and from there he found a main road, then hailed a cab.

When he opened the door to Mrs. Duncan's rooming house he was still drunk and stoned. His pant legs were wet from the snow and his face had scratches from the branches that had snapped across his cheeks and brow as he ran through the woods, Dr. Bluette on his trail. Cobb was in the second floor kitchen building another bomb, this one with gasoline and frozen orange juice. He stopped his work when he saw Will skulk past the kitchen on his way to his attic bedroom.

"What the hell happened to you?" he asked.

"I went to see a doctor," Will said as he climbed stairs to the attic and shut the door behind him.

REAL ESTATE

ANY MARKET IS UNPREDICTABLE. Nobody can say for sure when an Act of God is going to occur — one of those dreaded things in Florida that bankrupt insurance companies — but they happen in every market. There comes a time in a market when a necessary decision must be made. They're usually instigated by an Act of God, some unforeseen calamity for which no amount of risk analysis can account. The Royal Canadian Mounted Police were the Act of God that occurred in the west-Toronto cigarette market. How they got onto Cobb was anyone's guess. He knew them to have good skills when they had a scent, but they were inept at knowing where to look for scents. The appearance of the two officers at the Dolphin definitely constituted their discovery of a scent. Cobb had no choice but to make this clear to Will. They were partners and it was wrong to lie about risk to your partner. It led to bad communication and mistrust. Cobb knew dozens of convicts who were in jail because of bad partners. Theirs was a relationship that required complete trust.

Will digested the information Cobb gave him. He pondered the necessary decision that had to be made. Cobb knew it was Will's to make. They owned oxygen. They owned thousands of hectares of rain forest. They owned a half dozen small apartment buildings with full tenancy. Cobb didn't have to work on the sewers anymore. He had told Paddy that he had found a handyman job with a small property management company. All Paddy needed was a letter for his records, so Will had Mr. Kenny write it up. Cobb started to live by his own clock. But now it was Will's decision to make.

Will thought about it for one day and one night. Cobb allowed no more time. The RCMP were thorough and meticulous once they had a scent. This meant that Will's primary revenue stream was to end, they were to be entirely dependent on secondary earning models: the rent they took in minus mortgage payments, the earnings Mr. Kenny made, the marijuana and the punishment. The rent and the punishment covered their costs, but now that Cobb had another revenue stream, Will had some other things going as well.

He had land surveyors to chart and map the land he and Cobb had purchased, and, when they were done, he had Miguel Sanchez, *abrigado y notario*, serve the various government departments with legal papers, forcing them to process land grants they had promised at various earth summits. The grant money they were supposed to be giving out had been donated by the first world nations.

The local governments were a problem. They put up endless amounts of red tape and talked nonsense to delay the awarding of conservation grants to foreigners. Sanchez, however, was good, persistent and well connected. The grants started to come in; but, with the expense of surveyors and bribes to government officials deducted, their profit was only seventy percent of what Will had forecast. It was still profit.

Will's reasoning was thorough. He looked at all the activities of 1109897 Ontario Inc. from every angle. He even recalled in his attic musings the first known economic collaboration in Canada between the Europeans and Indians, the coureurs-de-bois, as Cobb had called him. They were Frenchmen who left the king's colonies under threat of prosecution by the king, and went into the bush with the Indians to become entrepreneurs in the fur trade, ignoring the king's declared right to the monopoly. Together, the coureurs and the Indians explored farther and chartered North America. The collaboration worked. The Indians respected the courage of the runners, their ability to give up their world and live as Indians and, once the coureurs were living with the Indians, they were little more than Indians with the memories of Europeans. The coureurs respected the knowledge of the Indians, their direct involvement with the environment and the insight this gave them. There were many parallels to the present situation. Cobb had been arrested once before. He had gone to jail. He had been the subject of an investigation before. His cautious suggestion to make haste with the rest of the inventory, to avoid being found with product, rang true to Will. He had no other counsel to take. Will had never been investigated by the RCMP and Cobb was the only person he knew who had. All risk was peril if even a small chance existed that Cobb could go back to jail. Will made his decision.

"We'll liquidate all inventory in the next twenty-four hours. Allow the buyer to set price based on volume. We have to liquidate," he told Cobb.

It was a large task. Their total inventory was in excess of three thousand cartons of cigarettes. There was little, if any, sentiment in the passing of their core business. It had served them well. The monthly dividend on the Polski portfolio was substantial, as were the revenue streams in marijuana and punishment. They would soon put the cigarettes and the revenue they generated out of their minds.

"'Real" comes from Latin, *realis*, meaning 'actual,' and 'realize' is from the French *realiser*, meaning, 'make real,'" Will said to Cobb, who drove the truck. Their last task was to go to cancel the lease on the garage where they stored the cigarettes.

"The word reality doesn't even come into documented existence until 1550, at which time it means fixed wealth," Will went on, "and this," he said, "has led me to conclude that Mr. Kenny is right. We should move more into real estate. Property could possibly take us into a revenue stream comparable to the cigarettes in our domestic market. We live here and there's money to be made. We don't need any more business than that. We're capitalized to go into this market right now. We can secure four more properties. Besides," Will added, "we could devolve the cigarette business to contractors. We have supply and the market is there. Maybe it's time we took our hands off that business in a direct way. I'm sure we could retain sixty percent of the business even if we transferred operations to contractors."

Cobb wanted nothing more to do with the cigarettes. He had a bad feeling about the cigarette business, nothing could change his mind and Will felt it only fair to allow him his say; after all, where God can act, intuition is sometimes the best logic. It was all sound economics to Will.

LOVE YOU

WILL AND PERSEY SAT in the Dolphin, sipping coffee and waiting for their eggs. It had been a while since they had seen one another. Will was in no mood to see her after the Easter Saturday dinner fiasco. He felt betrayed by having her declare to her mother that she was pregnant while he was there, without any forewarning that she was going to do it. He felt used; though when he tried to define how, his mind came up blank. Sometimes feelings can become thoughts by themselves, he figured, and maybe there didn't have to be any reason. He hadn't returned any of Persey's phone calls until this Saturday morning — and she had been calling almost every day since Easter. She felt very guilty about how the dinner had played out, the awkwardness of the whole thing for Will. What more was there to say between he and her mother after she dropped a bombshell like, "I'm pregnant?"

"Oh, shit," she said. "I'm sorry. I had no right to do that to you."

"No, you didn't."

"Can you forgive me?"

"I already have."

"Why did it take you so long to call me back then?"

"I don't know."

"You must know."

"I guess I just don't want to say then."

"Why not?"

"Persey, I agreed to have breakfast with you because I didn't want to leave you with a bad feeling. I don't want you to feel bad about what happened. You know, she's your mother. I have a family I've spoken to once in ten and a half months. There's nothing unique about your situation. We all have our stuff to deal with, and that's why I wanted to see you. I just wanted to see you so you would know that I don't have any bad feeling about you or about what happened. I just don't think we should see each other anymore."

"Why not?" she asked, genuinely distraught. The thought of rejection was too overwhelming for her, as though his casting her aside was the final straw in the internal war for her self-esteem.

"You're going to have a baby. Why complicate things?"

"What's complicated about being my friend?"

"You know what I mean."

The food came and Dorothy asked, "Ham?"

"Me," Persey said.

Dorothy placed the ham and eggs in front of Persey and the bacon and eggs in front of Will. She snapped a piece of gum. "Everything good then?" she asked.

"Yes," Will said.

"More coffee?" she asked, not willing to take his yes at face value — customers always wanted something. They just didn't know how to ask.

"Sure, yes," Will said. "A refill would be great."

"I seen him drink nine cups of coffee in an hour and a half one time," Dorothy said to Persephone, who nodded her head and smiled bemusedly at Will. Dorothy went on, "He sits in that back booth sometimes and reads for hours. He's a real bookworm this one." And that was the last of her commentary. She left them to eat in peace.

Will bent his head down and chewed slowly, enjoying his food and the diversion from the crippling conversation that had started to make him feel guilty. He didn't know why he felt guilty. He had done nothing wrong. There was no reason to feel guilty; but, as he had deduced already, sometimes a feeling is the beginning of a thought without meaning. This made him think the guilt was reasonable. After all, if he couldn't trust his feelings what could he trust? How could a feeling lie? People think themselves into lies.

"Why didn't you want to sleep with me?" Persey asked.

Will looked into her face. His mouth was open. He didn't know what to say. She moved her head to look over his left shoulder. His back was to the door. She held her eyes over his shoulder for a moment or two, then moved her eyes in a way that suggested that he should look over his shoulder, and so he did. Paddy was standing behind him in his pink housecoat, bare underneath, his pale and flaky skin exposed. Will looked down and he had his rabbit ear slippers on his feet. It was freezing outside. Paddy's eyes were red and puffy. He had been crying.

"I love you, Will," he said.

"What the hell are you talking about, Paddy?"

BLACK CAT

COBB AGREED TO FEED Fatima's cat. He noted some odd phenomena inside his head when he was alone in the house with it. He had flashes in his mind's eye: the cat run over by a car, the cat weighted and thrown into the lake, the cat frozen in an alley, like Polski.

The trick for coping with malevolent imagination is non-participation. While most people regard their interiors as their sovereign province, Cobb knew that the interior is just another place. It had to be respected in the same way the earth had to be respected. He had to make his peace with Crow, but Crow would not come to his dream and talk to him. He knew he should just walk away from the black cat, but he couldn't. Fatima loved the cat. Crow was jealous. Crow could be chased away by love, and Cobb would be left to the black robes. There was no disputing a dream. The anger that had grown in Cobb when he was in the corrections system could only be taken away by a period of service to Crow, and service to Crow required fidelity to Crow. The surrender of love, the peace of it, it was the Crow's right. Every party to a contract has rights, especially if the contract is made in a dream.

Cobb knew that he had to remain allied with Crow; however, in his heart, he wanted to stay with Fatima's black cat. He didn't know what to do. The black cat caused him no end of anguish for several days and nights, until Crow decided to stop laughing at him and visited him in a dream.

In the dream Crow was on a branch. The black cat was perched below it. The black cat was fixated on Crow, and Crow was smiling — Cobb knew the expression represented a smile, and that it represented knowledge and cunning. Crow swooped and the black cat pounced; but, just as luck becomes cats in balance, it deferred to Crow where death was concerned. The black cat realized mid-pounce that it was not going to get Crow. It landed on its paws and turned around for the next leap. Crow was right in front of it, taunting it. The black cat was proud. It is a fatal flaw in Crow's adversary. The black cat pounced and Crow moves again. The cat landed right in front of a car. Everything went black for a moment. There was an awful sound. Cobb saw the red smear on the asphalt and Crow picking at the innards.

Cobb woke with a shock. He dressed and walked quickly over to Fatima's building. It was just past noon.

When he got there, the door was off the frame. He pushed the door open slowly, not knowing what to expect. There were wood splinters on the floor of the foyer. The door had been kicked in. A psychic reading shop and a dungeon — the list of people who knew about it was long. He stood silently in the foyer, breathing through his nose. There was nobody in the house. He could sense it. The bad spirit was gone. The power of Crow was back, the guidance and protection of Crow was back. He closed his eyes and there was no flash. He was as clear as a snow-covered field.

The cat was gone. This was bad.

Cobb had to find the cat before it came to harm. He cursed himself for falling in love with Fatima. He was in deep now. Fortunately, Cobb was a good tracker and there was a way to track a domesticated cat in a city. All was not lost.

Cobb bolted up the stairs. He looked into the kitchen. The food and water dishes were on the floor, where he had last seen them. They were not empty. The cat didn't come out of any of the other upstairs rooms, as it usually did when it heard him.

Cobb tumbled down the stairs to the dungeon, where the cat was known to lie, sleeping, or occasionally kill a mouse. By day, the dungeon appeared ludicrous. The whips, the shackles, the suspension riggings, the ball gags, the masks, the beautiful bear skin, they all looked like toys, not the instruments of pain and fear by which Cobb had brought grown men to tears. The cat was nowhere to be seen.

Cobb's next step was to circle the perimeter of the property. He had to look for droppings, although cats were notoriously efficient at cleaning up after themselves. He also had to figure out which way the cat would have gone if it left the yard. He had to think like the cat. What are its needs? Given that this was an indoor cat, what things on the street would change its direction, cause it fear or hesitation? Would it allow itself to be touched by people? Probably, Cobb thought with some horror. It had known nothing but love and trust from people.

Cobb decided he would move to the main street. The cat would go there for the garbage in front of the shops. He wondered if the cat would wander that far from its home. It was hard to say. When he came out of the alley he almost bumped into an old woman in black. The sidestep Cobb performed saved her from his speeding form, but sent him shoulder-first into an unsuspecting white man, a white-shirted white man with a briefcase, who was sent spinning to the ground. With a look of genuine concern on his face, Cobb moved quickly to aid the man. He was sorry. Very sorry. Accidents were omens to Cobb; and he behaved accordingly, seeking the goodwill of the victim, hoping to cure quickly any hard feelings that might come to a curse, but the man skidded backward on his pants, a look of mortal fear on his face, a huge Indian moving in on him like a predatory animal.

Cobb scooped up the man's briefcase and held it up the way he would hold up a food offering to an animal he didn't know, a simple form of communication that means peace and trust.

"Hey, buddy," Cobb said, stepping toward him in long strides, "You lost your briefcase."

The man stayed down on the sidewalk like a beaten animal. "No. No. Keep it."

Cobb reached down and picked the man up, seemingly against his will. Cobb stood him erect and brushed some dirt off the shoulders of the man's suit. The man was petrified. Cobb handed him the briefcase and smiled warmly, touching the man on the shoulder in genuine good will.

"Sir," Cobb said. "That was entirely my fault. I hope you can forgive me. I was very rude."

The man looked suddenly dumbfounded. "That's all right, sir," he said to Cobb. "Accidents happen."

Cobb and the white man parted amicably, with no curse upon Cobb. The old woman was gone. It was a sign. Cobb had to find her.

He looked both ways down the street. She was gone. One moment she was almost immobile and the next she had disappeared. Cobb glanced across the street. There was no way she could have crossed the street. The traffic was too thick. Where did she get to? He went back to the last place he had seen her, right in front of the narrow alley from which he had just sped into the frightened man. He walked over to the alley and looked into it. There she was. And, to his relief, she had the cat.

The cat had followed Cobb into the alley. He had been right about the cat's motivation. It had headed for the garbage. He had only overestimated how far it had travelled. When the cat saw Cobb, it tracked him on its silent, padded feet. But now the old woman had the cat. This was no accident. Cobb stepped back and faded into the crowded sidewalk so that when the woman came out of the alley with the cat, she wouldn't see Cobb. This is precisely what happened; the old woman in black came out of the alley and turned right, the black cat cradled in her arms.

The old woman moved slowly down Queen Street. She wore a long winter jacket, a shawl over her head and big waterproof boots. She stopped every so often to rest. It took her twenty minutes to walk a block. She was in her own world. She did not know Cobb was stalking her.

Things got trickier. Cobb saw the white woman he had copulated with at the Gladstone eight months earlier, the head-shrinker with the scars on her wrist. She was coming down the street. She had a moon in her belly. He ducked into a doorway and brought a newspaper up to his face, peeking out enough just to maintain surveillance. He saw Persey see the old woman in black and go white with fear. She crossed the street quickly and headed away from the old woman, not once looking back. Cobb had the feeling they knew each other.

The old woman walked to the side of the road. To Cobb's shock and horror, she tossed the cat into the street, where it was crushed under the wheel of a passing bus, unable to regain its composure quickly enough to dart out of the tire's way. Cobb took no vengeance. The old woman had to be an agent of Crow. The signs were all around him.

WINNING TICKET

FATIMA WAS DISTURBED BY the disappearance of the black cat. She put the punishment business on hold. The cat had been gone for some time. Fatima accepted the fact that her cat was gone, but she took it as a bad omen. She stopped having sex with Cobb. She had felt uncomfortable with him since the cat disappeared. Cobb missed the sex, and he missed her company. He hadn't known this kind of pain in quite a while. The situation made him anxious. After a week of not hearing from Fatima, he had gone over to her place, but she was not there. She had gone up north, and might not be returning. Another revenue stream had dried up.

Cobb had to keep busy, so he went over to Paddy's apartment and down the stairs to the mailboxes at the end of the hall. He glanced around quickly to make sure nobody was watching, then he opened up Paddy's box and went through the letters. There was a letter to him from Allied Insurance: Life's Necessities. He put the envelope inside his jacket and the others back in Paddy's box, which he locked up. He sprinted up the stairs and returned home. In the second floor kitchen, he tore the envelope open and read.

Re: Policy #CB1102-044D
Dear Mr. Seymour:

We regret to inform you that Policy #CB1102-044D is void. The insured, Martin Fischer, is a diagnosed schizophrenic and a ward of the Public Trustee. He is currently resident at the Queen Street location of the Centre for Addiction and Mental Health.

Although the premiums for the last nine months have been paid in full, we have voided this policy as you failed to inform us of Mr. Fischer's pre-existing illnesses. The forms, which you signed, clearly require that all illnesses must be reported. Failure to comply renders this policy void. We will not be refunding your payments.

Further inquiries may be directed to our solicitors, Gerber and Feak.

Sincerely,
Jason Clark

Cobb pounced from the table and marched to the telephone. He knew the number by heart and dialled it. It rang twice.

"Alexander Campbell?" Cobb asked.

He waited two minutes, then the voice came on, "Alexander Campbell here."

"Randall Seymour here. I —"

"Randall I can't talk to you ever again."

"Ah, cut the shit, Campbell. I have some lawyering for you to do."

"Randall, I couldn't possibly represent you in any matter ever again."

"I have a cash retainer."

"How much?"

"What do you need?"

STONE

WILL SAT IN A booth at the Dolphin. 1109897 Ontario Inc. had little for him to do. The cigarettes were gone, the punishment was gone, the weed was gone. He didn't have to collect rent on the buildings he and Cobb owned. Mr. Kenny had set payments up on automatic withdrawal. He and Mr. Kenny did not go to lunch anymore, they rarely spoke on the phone. The flow of cash had levelled off, then declined. Mr. Kenny had inquired about the dispersals from the primary trust, and Will informed him that the trustees were giving him no explanations. "It's all smoke and mirrors with the primary trust," he told Mr. Kenny.

Will had no new ideas about where to take 1109897 Ontario Inc. He felt disconnected from the world. His hair was unkempt and he was growing another thin beard. He couldn't understand how his vision had brought him to the place he now occupied. He sat in the Dolphin for hours every day, reading newspapers and watching the news on Fred's TV. The world was little more than a corporation, he realized in those weeks of idleness. The world was so dark. He could barely live with himself.

Will closed the newspaper and stared blankly at Dorothy. It had become dangerous for him to look at the world. The lightness and optimism that had commenced his journey to his vision had become as heavy and immovable as stone. It was an unsettling thing to see the same season twice under the ambiguity of the same vision, and spring was upon him. There was a sense of redundancy and futility in his life.

His internal economy was in turmoil and in that turmoil he saw the turmoil of the world, of its economy. The loss of reasoning, the hardening of the imagination, which was fuelled, to Will's mind, by the delicate human hope that the light of the species will prevail — not once and finally, but daily and forever, against the forces of ignorance and fear. He was losing faith in himself and faith in the world. He was losing faith that the experts would lead all people to a better standard of living. How could there be any standard of living where there was no standard of existence? When things went wrong, as they seemed to be more and more, the human species tore up its invisible lottery ticket and cursed itself a fool for believing in the first place. There is not enough to go around.

The only real fear in the known universe was the fear of the human species, the childlike fear of an unstructured imagination, a purposeless existence. The only proof it sought was that existence was not the product of random forces.

Will had to hold to his vision's course, whatever that might be, because it was a question of liability. He had been given the vision, which, according to Cobb, was a sacred thing that became the responsibility of the seer. This was the real economy, Will concluded: the economy of vision, the internal workings of a human being, with no boundaries put on it.

Will realized he had to talk and, because Robert Polski had disappeared again, he knew there was only one person he could talk to — Paddy.

He stood and dropped a few dollars on the table, between the dirty dishes with egg yolk, bread crusts and tomato slices. He left the Dolphin and crossed the road. He went down the stairs, down the dingy hallway, and knocked on Paddy's door. There was no movement on the other side. Maybe Paddy was out walking the dog. He knocked again, with more force, and the door pushed open a couple of inches.

"Paddy," he said. There was no answer.

He pushed the door all the way back and saw Paddy on the floor, a kind of purple colour, his eyes hollow and glassy.

"Oh —"

He walked into the bathroom, following the sound of a soft whimpering. King was on the floor. He was languid and sad. He hardly moved, hardly looked up at Will.

Will left the bathroom and looked at the things on the coffee table, scanning for the note or letter that people leave behind to give some insight into their state of mind. He found it on the coffee table, right beside a big envelope.

Dear Will,

There are some days that I see no beauty in the world. On these days, I'm okay. There are other days when there is beauty in the world. On these days, I'm not. I have decided to end my journey. My accomplishments are not impressive. I leave nobody behind. My struggle in the world has not amounted to much. What little there is, I give to you. You have given me hope. You caused me to consider things I had allowed myself to forget. For this, and more, I'm grateful. I love you.

Paddy

Will opened the larger envelope. It was full of money. He counted it out quickly. About eighty thousand dollars. He fell to the floor and curled up in the fetal position, softly whimpering, a human imitation of the dog's behaviour in the bathroom. He stayed like this for a long time, then fell asleep.

Cobb woke him up.

"Paddy loved you?"

"Apparently so," Will sniffled and coughed. He sat himself upright on the floor.

"It's okay, Will," Cobb said. "He was dying anyway."

"AIDS?"

"Cancer."

"He never told me."

"No matter. He traded well for the queen. He kept his word. He had honour."

Cobb grabbed the big envelope and removed twelve thousand dollars.

"This is mine," he said. "I loaned him twelve thousand dollars when I got out of prison."

"I was going to put it all in the company, anyways," Will said.

"What do you want to do?" Cobb asked.

"Well, we're not going to burn Paddy?"

"No," Cobb said. "We can't burn Paddy."

"What then?"

"Nothing. We do nothing," Cobb said. "Grab the note and the cash. We don't want to be questioned about this."

"What about the dog?"

"They'll take care of him when they find him," Cobb said.

"They'll kill him," Will said.

"Maybe," Cobb said. "But there's nothing we can do about that. If the dog's gone they'll know the scene's been tampered with. We have to leave the dog."

They left the apartment. In his mind Will recited — a stream, a bright light, a crow, a black bear, a crucifix, a stone and purple flowers.

DEPARTURES

WILL WAS LEFT TO attend to Paddy. He made an anonymous call to the medical examiner's office. They sent an ambulance some hours later. The animal authorities had to sedate King with a tranquilizer gun. He wasn't willing to leave the apartment. He wasn't willing to go anywhere without his master. He couldn't understand that his master would never go anywhere again. A dog has the luxury of never having to think about death, never having to actualize death, but when death comes they're blindsided. Who could say, Will thought, how many masters leave the earth before their animals, and who knew what happened to all of these animals, if there was any study of their feelings, their behaviour? It didn't matter. He and Cobb had seen sadness in King, and he and Cobb knew that the animal felt in a way similar to people. They had made it real by sharing. Still, it was a horrible sight to see the large dog brought out, his head flopping and his paws limp and dangling.

The smell of Paddy's death must have been horrible. King must have had some sense of what the smell meant. That simple understanding, with no defense for it, no way to express or expel the grief, must have been horrible for King. Will didn't know why he kept thinking about King. It was probably because he didn't want to think about Paddy, who hadn't been brought out of the building yet. A group of about twenty people had gathered outside. The ambulance was a natural curiosity for them. There were a few of the street's children, including the little girl he had seen blowing soap bubbles in the spring, shortly after he had moved into Mrs. Duncan's rooming house. The year had made significant changes in her appearance. She looked more grown up. She was with a group of kids, some Will recognized and some he didn't, and the older ones had a hard edge to their looks and actions, the next generation of work for people like Paddy Pape.

Mrs. Duncan had come out of her house as well. It was a rare street appearance for one of the few property owners on the street. Aside from walking to church on Sunday mornings, she lived as though there were a contract out on her life, rarely leaving the first floor of her house. The commotion had proved too much for her to resist, so there she was — slack-jawed and wide-eyed like everyone else, Dorothy had left her post at the Dolphin and she wanted to know: Is it the queer in the basement apartment? AIDS? Was he robbed and killed? Did they kill his dog? A good number of the drunks from the Dolphin were on the street as well, leaving their cheap draft for a few moments to see the commotion. Will felt like crap. He felt like there was a tear in his stomach, like he was going to soil his pants, like he was going to fall down and cry.

Finally the stretcher came up the stairs. There were two paramedics at the back and one at the front. Paddy was fat and heavy. He never seemed like a big man to Will. He seemed regular, but the strain of the men lifting the stretcher up the stairs broke that illusion for Will. Paddy was immense. The white sheet was pulled up over him, the universal sign that the patient is dead. As the two men at the back pushed up on the stretcher to clear the last few steps, the man in the front lost his bearing and fell backward. This went unseen by the two paramedics at the back, who continued to push without the guidance of the front man. The stretcher turned to its side, hung in the air for moment, then tumbled over and with it Paddy Pape, naked, bloated, purple and stiff. There was a gasp in the crowd. The children looked on with stunned expressions. A few of the older children, probably around twelve, just before puberty but way past malice, laughed. The paramedics rushed to restore dignity to the cadaver. They rolled Paddy in the white sheet and then lifted him back onto the stretcher.

Will caught Dorothy out of the corner of his eye. She had moved close to him and now stood right beside Mrs. Duncan, who had turned to Dorothy when the body had fallen. They had exchanged words, which culminated with Dorothy pointing at Will, saying loud enough for him and others to hear, "That one there was his boyfriend."

Will put his head down and departed.

CROW

WILL WAS DEVASTATED BY the passing of Paddy Pape. He'd never known anyone who had died. He stayed in his room all day and night. He took no food. Cobb asked him if he was going to fast again, as he had done the previous spring, and Will told him he didn't know, he just didn't feel like eating.

With no cigarettes to deliver and no punishment to be dealt out, yet a steady stream of money coming into the company from the dream economy, Cobb found himself lethargic. He wondered if Crow was finished with him. Like William Tobe, he lost his will to eat. They both stayed in their rooms and fasted another day and night. Cobb refused to lie down on his bed. He sat in the centre of his room. He drifted in and out of sleep, like a fevered man. He received his final instructions from Crow.

In his dream it was winter, but Cobb was not cold. The air was chill, the ground frozen. He was in the woods. He did not know how long he had to wait for an elder, and so he built himself a small fire. He placed his hands over the fire and rubbed them together. He waited and waited, but the elder did not come. He heard dogs. He saw Crow in the air. Crow was circling. His black wings were wide and his cry horrible. Crow made wider and wider circles in the sky. Cobb watched carefully. Something was being spoken to him. Crow moved closer to an island on the far side of the frozen and snow-covered lake. Cobb knew he must go to the island. There was a moment of hesitation. He knew what the island means. The island is alone, a place of death. He wondered if Crow was leading him to his death. It didn't matter. He had to follow Crow. He was bonded to Crow. He walked onto the lake. The ice beneath his feet was strong. There was no danger. He began to walk more swiftly. He stopped looking to the sky for guidance. He knew Crow would be waiting for him. The sound of the dogs was gone. There was nothing following him, nothing tracking him. The snow was deep. The closer he got to the island, the deeper the snow was. At the rock shore of the island the snow was up to his waist and the wind was strong, howling around him. It seized the snow and brushed against his face. He pushed up the shore and onto the island, where he heard the wretched lament of Crow. He walked toward the sound. He moved through the wooded island, the dense brush, the evergreens, thicker and heavier in the winter, the snow and ice holding to them. At centre of the island, William Tobe was in the clearing. He was shivering and frightened. Crow was gone, no sight or sound of Crow.

Cobb said, "William Tobe, what are you doing here?"

Will shrugged his shoulders, holding himself in an effort to retain warmth. Cobb saw his need and responded to it. He gathered twigs and made a fire. Will joined him beside the fire warmed his hands. Cobb left the fire and to gather evergreen branches for them to sit on, so that they could rest beside the fire without getting wet.

Cobb and Will sat silently, until Cobb asked, "How did you come to this place?"

Will answered, "I don't know."

"This is a death place, Will."

Will became frightened.

Cobb looked warmly at him and told him that an island in winter is a natural death for the weak and the elderly, the ones the tribe can no longer care for. The cold is a good and peaceful way to slip into the death world, to pass from the body for good. The person left on the island has only to fall asleep. Freezing to death is very peaceful, Cobb told him. It is a very human way to leave the world because there is very little suffering. "The person sleeps and dreams," Cobb told him. "And then death walks into the dream, quietly and peacefully, and the dream of life is taken into the dream of death, and the person hardly knows the difference."

Will was warm. He liked the story. Cobb heard Crow on the edge of the island, the place he had stepped onto the island. He knew he had to leave. He told Will to fall asleep by the fire. He wished him a peaceful journey.

Cobb woke up knowing Crow was finished with him. He had been let go.

Cobb went up to the attic. He walked through the door and shook Will awake. It was 4:30 a.m.

"I had a dream," Cobb said.

"Huh?" Will said.

"Our dreams have crossed, Will, and Crow has given me permission to give you direction on your vision."

Will sat bolt upright. "You know about the crow?" he said.

"I can't speak about your vision, Will. I can only give you instruction on how to understand your vision."

"When?"

"We must make all our plans now. Crow is finished with me. Crow has told me to leave this place."

LAST RITES

It was the day they were going to bury Paddy Pape. Will woke before dawn and packed just two bags, clothes and books. It was amazing how little he owned. Cobb, too, had little. He had left the house the day after they found Paddy. He only had a duffel bag over his shoulder. Will had dressed himself in a fine dark suit and silk tie. He had cut his hair and shaved.

He looked out the little square window in his room. Although it was raining, it was warm enough to open it and stick his head out, the way he had done when he had first taken the room. He was leaving shortly after Paddy's arrangements had been made. He was to take the truck up north. Cobb had bought some property in the woods. He wanted the truck left there. After that, Will had to settle his vision once and for all. Will had been living in Toronto almost a year.

He went over to the Dolphin for coffee. He took Cobb's small black bag with him.

The rain brought back the memory of his vision. His deepest reflections on the vision had been in the previous rain-soaked spring when he had arrived from Ottawa. It had been so long since he had spoken to his sister. His family must miss him, he thought. He had been mourning Paddy Pape's passing for three and a half days. He had been mourning as Cobb had instructed him to mourn. He woke every morning at dawn and walked to the lake. He spoke to the lake, the trees and the sky. He spoke to the Creator.

This was Will's his first appearance in the Dolphin in more than a week.

Robert Polski entered, walked to his booth and sat down. Robert had been gone for some time. Now Cobb was gone. Paddy was gone. But Robert was back. Will ordered him breakfast.

"That's a nice suit, Will," Robert said.

"Thanks, Robert."

"You look like an economist."

Will sat stupefied in front of Robert. Somewhere in the seemingly random images that had played themselves out in his head a year past were the answers to how he came to be the heir to Paddy Pape's estate, guardian of the resurrected Robert Polski, and partner in 1109897 Ontario Inc. His life had become the vision he couldn't define. Who were these people?

Will suddenly said goodbye to Robert and left the Dolphin. He went home and sat in his chair in front of the attic window for some time, staring at the grey and desolate day. He held a police badge that had been waiting for him on the porch, along with a note from Philmore, saying he could no longer hold onto it because Fatima had left Cobb.

No funeral was arranged. They were going to cremate Paddy. Those were his wishes. All that remained for Will to do was visit the funeral home and sign the registry. Will put the badge in the inside pocket of his suit jacket and left his room.

Will went to the Royal Bank, where he was greeted by Mr. Kenny. It turned out that Mr. Kenny had been managing Paddy's money for a little longer than he had 1109897 Ontario Inc.'s — small world. Mr. Kenny had received a letter days before Paddy was found. It instructed him to contact William Tobe. It was odd for Mr. Kenny and Will to meet under such circumstances. Once the automatic withdrawals form 1109897 Ontario Inc. had stabilized, there had been no need for them to communicate. It was a solemn occasion, the greetings were terse. Mr. Kenny put on his overcoat and left of the bank with Will. A light rain fell, nothing more than a heavy mist. It couldn't be felt, but, after six blocks of walking, both Will and Mr. Kenny were wet. On the way to the funeral home they discussed 1109897 Ontario Inc.'s year-end reporting. Will had signed all the papers. He was the president of the corporation. The retained earnings of 1109897 Ontario Inc. were just in excess of $750,000. They arrived at the funeral home and walked into the foyer, where they were greeted almost immediately by a dour-looking man in a dark suit.

"Paddy Pape," Will said.

They were led to a dimly lit room in which Paddy Pape lay in a wooden box. The arrangements had been seen to by Mr. Kenny.

It was like a dream, Will and Mr. Kenny standing before the corpse of Paddy Pape, hands folded in front of them, saying nothing. The silence was loud. Funeral homes were built to accommodate silence, and silence was an accommodation in a city. There was no priest or minister to say a few words.

Will stepped forward and said, "This man I knew, Paddy Pape, he was a good man. He wanted to leave the world a better place than he found it. He never gave up on people and he never stopped loving life. He dreamed of a better world and, like a jealous lover, the world that is took its revenge. He taught me that compassion comes from the passions." Will reached into his black bag and removed a purple carnation. He placed it atop the coffin, then he stepped back and bowed his head.

After what he felt was a suitable time of reflection on the impromptu eulogy, Mr. Kenny whispered in front of Paddy Pape's coffin; he told Will that if the dispersals from the primary trust picked up again it was quite possible for the company to make a million dollars in its second year. Will explained, also in whisper, that the larger dispersals were the result of money released after litigation, and that the bulk of it had been given to Mr. Polski. However, Will whispered, there was just recently another transfer from the primary trust, in fact, the biggest ever, a quarter of a million dollars, the result of an out-of-court settlement on a dispute within the primary trust beneficiaries.

"A quarter of a million dollars?" Mr. Kenny said.

"A quarter of a million dollars," Will said, and handed the cheque, which he had signed in the taxi on the way to the Royal Bank, to Mr. Kenny.

Mr. Kenny looked it over.

"Who is Randall Seymour?" he asked.

"He's a cousin of Mr. Polski's."

"I see," Mr. Kenny said.

Will and Mr. Kenny signed the registry on the way out. They both noted with slight discomfort that they were the only people to have come to the home. There was no family, no other friends.

Will made arrangements with Mr. Kenny for the management of 1109897 Ontario Inc., as he would be leaving Toronto for an undetermined period of time. He wanted to make sure that the corporation would be taken care of.

Mr. Kenny returned to the bank and Will continued on.

Will walked home slowly through the drizzle. Once he got there, he climbed the stairs to the attic and retrieved the notebook computer. He brought it down to the kitchen, ran the phone cord around the corner, plugged it into the computer's modem, and checked his e-mail. Cobb was in Costa Rica. His e-mail said that he had surveyed the land. Some locals had wined and dined him and they wanted him to invest in a big banana operation, which they said they could get off the ground for a quarter million US dollars. In his reply e-mail, Will asked Cobb to have the locals e-mail a prospectus in English, or some kind of formal business plan with risk and return projections, otherwise, it would not be possible. But they both agreed that banana farming might not be a bad business.

After the e-mail Will went back upstairs. He lay down on his mattress in the attic and promptly fell asleep.

Sometime later there was a knock on the front door. He didn't hear Mrs. Duncan's footsteps. The knock sounded again and again, louder and louder. Who the hell would do that? he wondered. He got up, dressed and padded down the stairs. By the time he got to the door, the person was knocking loud enough to wake the dead. Will pulled open the door and looked at the man in a dark suit and tie, who had a thick mustache, and who was holding a briefcase. He was a cop. Will knew it the moment he saw him.

"What do you want?" Will asked.

"Is Randall Seymour here?"

"Who?"

"Randall Seymour."

"Never heard of him."

"Our records show that he lived here from November of last year."

"What records? Who are you?"

"My name is DaCosta, Frank DaCosta. I'm a detective sergeant with the RCMP."

He reached into his jacket and removed his badge. Will had never seen an RCMP badge before. They were actually quite regal.

"What do you want?"

"I'm trying to locate Randall Seymour. He's a convicted felon. His parole record indicates that he lives here, but we have no record of his whereabouts since his parole officer passed away."

"Well, like I said. I never heard of him."

"I must advise you that it would be in Randall's best interests to contact my office."

"Look, buddy, you're the one who lost a felon, not me, so don't give me any of your strong-arm shit, okay? I've got half a mind to call my city councillor and my member of the provincial parliament and tell them the RCMP came to my door to warn me that there was a convicted felon lost in my neighbourhood. How long did you say you've been missing this guy, Frank? A day? A week? Are you going door-to-door, Frank? How did you end up at my door? What makes you think a person I've never heard of has been living in this house? Do you want to step in and look at the unclaimed mail? This is a rooming house, you know, there's always a record of people in a rooming house."

"If you lie to me, you could be charged with obstructing justice."

"Fuck you, asshole. What are you going to do, pepper spray me? You have no grounds for an arrest, nor would you be in a position to secure an arrest at my home without a specific subsection on an arrest warrant, which you don't have, not to mention the fact that you haven't made anything clear about what justice you're serving by your presence here today, let alone what justice you've observed obstructed. Do you mean 'law' when you say 'justice?' That would make more sense, only then we'd have to dispute interpretations of the law, because the law includes my rights — and chief among them is my right to knowledge and, more specifically, the 'justice' you have defined and how I might aid in your pursuit of it. Because I'm a citizen. Justice is important to me. A community can't function without justice. By the way, I'm curious, does that obstructing shit usually work in communities like this? I mean, how stupid do you count on people being to effectively do your job? Obstructing justice? You, sir, are one of the stupidest fucks I've met in some time."

"May I ask your name?"

"I'm the man who's going to save the world. If you want to keep breathing, you'll waste as little of my time as possible."

"Are you threatening me?"

"That's a matter of interpretation, and you don't have all the facts, and you've wasted enough of mine already. Now, unless you wish to proceed with an obstruction arrest, I'm closing my door."

"Good day, sir."

"I'll see you, Frank."

Will watched Detective Sergeant DaCosta walk down the chipped concrete steps, cross the patched asphalt street, get into his car, and drive away without so much as a glance back. Will went back upstairs and back to sleep.

He didn't know how long he'd been asleep. Outside the small square window in the attic, it was still gray, and it was still raining lightly. There was another knock at the door. He sat up on his mattress. He listened carefully. It wasn't the same knock. It was much lighter. He listened for the movements of Mrs. Duncan. She rarely answered the door. He decided that he wouldn't open the door. He lay down on his mattress. The knocking persisted. He didn't care who it was. He heard movement on the ground floor. Mrs. Duncan was up and about. If she answered the door and it was the Mountie he was in trouble. He lay on his back and waited.

He listened to Mrs. Duncan's slow footsteps make their way to the door. He heard voices. They were both female. He felt a deep relief. It could just be a door-to-door canvasser, Greenpeace, or something like that. There was no need to worry. He closed his eyes and tried to nap some more, but it was not to be. He heard the slow steps of Mrs. Duncan ascending the stairs, something she hadn't done since Cobb moved into her large home. He sat up again on his mattress, propped on his palms which were planted behind him. Will listened carefully. He heard her voice.

"Mr. Tobe," she called from the second floor landing.

He got up and cracked his door an inch.

"Yes?"

"Speak to the person at the door, please," she said.

"Okay," he said. He closed his door and went to the window. He looked around for the Mountie's car. He couldn't see it. He heard Mrs. Duncan walk back down the stairs and into her parlour. He opened his door and went down the three flights of stairs. The door was closed. Whoever was on the other side hadn't been invited into the house. He took a deep breath and opened the door. It was a woman. She looked to be in her early twenties, very rough around the edges. She had a lot of makeup on.

"I'm looking for Cobb," she said.

"Who are you?" Will asked.

"Sheila. Me an him lived in the Gladstone."

"Cobb's gone."

"He said he was gonna leave an envelope for me."

"There's no envelope," Will said.

"Is he gonna mail it?"

"I don't know."

"I need that envelope."

"I can't help you, Sheila."

"I need that envelope."

"I can't help you."

"Maybe he mailed it."

"If he did, it wouldn't be mailed here."

"Where would he mail it?"

"Just a second. I'll get my jacket and we can go check."

Will put on his suit jacket and he and Sheila walked the ten blocks to the property where 1109897 Ontario Inc. received its mail. Cobb thought it was better to receive mail somewhere he didn't live. Will walked up the front steps with Sheila in tow and knocked on the door.

PC Richard Chase opened the door and froze when he saw Sheila beside a clean-cut young man in a suit and tie. Discretion was a big part of her business as a prostitute, so she let him off the hook and just looked at the ground.

"Yes," he said.

"Oh, hello, I'm wondering if there's any mail for 1109897 Ontario Inc.?"

"You are?" Chase asked.

"A friend of the director's. He asked me to pick up his mail."

"I can't give you the mail, kid," Chase said. "It's from an insurance company. It might be a benefits cheque."

"Look, sir, my friend asked me to get his mail, that's all. There was no mention of the legality of it."

"Where's your friend?"

"Latin America."

"I see," Chase said, placing a hand under his chin.

"Just give him the fucking mail, pencil dick," Sheila said.

Persey heard the conversation from the living room where she was rocking the baby. Her memory placed the voice. It was William Tobe. The baby was asleep. She walked briskly to the front door to see whether or not her ears were playing tricks on her, and no, she hadn't been tricked. It was William Tobe.

She peeked out from behind Dick. He didn't move easily. It was like trying to push a big dog out of the way. She squeezed past him, smiled, said, "Hello, Will."

"Persey?"

"Yes, how are you?"

"I'm fine. You live here?"

"Yes. Why?"

"I'm a partner in the property management company that owns this building."

"You're kidding?"

"No. I had a little money. I invested it with a couple of friends. We picked the place up with a small down payment. It's self-sufficient."

Chase squeezed Persey's arm affectionately, gave her the letters and left the vestibule to go back and check on the baby. Persey handed him the letters Chase had left with her. She looked at Sheila and she looked at Will.

"Oh, this is Sheila," Will said.

"Nice to meet you," Persey said, and the two women shook hands.

"Well, as long as you're here, do you want to see the baby?" Persey asked.

"I'd love to," Will said.

Persey led Will and Sheila into the living room and beamed above the newborn in the rocker.

It was the oddest thing. He thought his mind was playing tricks on him. The baby looked exactly like Cobb. Will reached over and hugged her. Chase stepped toward them and the sound of his step told Will to let go of the baby. They looked at each other.

"I have to go," Will said. "Thanks for the mail."

He and Sheila walked to the vestibule. In half a second, Sheila slipped into her heels and she bolted outside. The door closed behind her. Will stooped to slip into his loafers and he heard Dick and Persey in the living room.

"There's no way that guy owns this property," Chase said." I just gave him the letters because I believe he knows the other guy, and because I wanted to avoid a confrontation. That guy was in a parking lot six blocks over last summer. Someone called it in. He was wandering around talking to himself and breaking bottles at midnight. He lives in a home. Real whack job. Jesus talk and everything. I remember that guy. It was just before I was assaulted. And that broad with him, she's a crack whore. She's been busted three times."

"Well, that would explain why he never let me pick him up at his house," Persey said. "I knew he was under a lot of stress, but I had no idea he was that unbalanced." She stood silent for a moment, then said, "It's so sad the way things turn out sometimes. There's just so much sadness in the world."

Will slipped out of the house quietly and let the door glide shut. Sheila was waiting for him on the sidewalk. Cars were slowing down as they passed her. She and Will went through the mail as they walked. There was nothing for her. She wouldn't leave Will without some kind of payment after learning he was Cobb's partner. He went to an ATM and got her $500. She wanted to suck his cock, but he told her he didn't want it. The last thing she said to him, as she was counting the money in an alley, was, "Am I high or did that fucking baby look like Cobb?"

On his way back to Mrs. Duncan's rooming house, for what would be his last night there, Will dropped the police badge of PC Richard Chase into a mailbox. It would crawl like a spider across the vast web of the queen's bureaucracy until it found the place it came from.

PURPLE FLOWERS

It was dark when the small alarm clock sounded. Will turned it off and sat up. He yawned and scratched his head, which reminded him he had cut his hair the day before. Most of it was gone. He scratched his chin and where there had once been a beard there was only thin stubble. He stood and turned on the light in the attic. His clothes were packed. His books were packed. He dressed. He picked up his bags and his notebook computer and descended the stairs slowly, like a pack animal on a narrow mountain passage, only his peril was not a fall to his death. His peril was waking Mrs. Duncan.

The truck was parked on the street. He stepped slowly down the front steps, down the wet footpath, across the sidewalk, across the street and to the truck. He loaded the bags into the cab. He put the notebook computer on the passenger seat. The lights were not on in the Dolphin. Fred hadn't even arrived yet. Up the road, a streetcar shuffled past. Will got into the truck and turned the key. He pumped the gas peddle and kept the key turned. He bent his head and said, "Come on, come on, come on." The engine turned over.

He sat up. Robert Polski was standing beside the truck, looking in. Will rolled down the window.

"You leaving, Will?"

"Yeah."

"You never told me."

"I'll be back."

"Those your bags, Will?"

"Yeah."

"You never told me you were leaving."

"I'll be back, Robert."

"When?"

"When I've found my vision in the world."

"Are you an economist, Will?"

"No, Robert. In the legal definition, I'm not an economist. I've never received salary or commission under that title."

"Are you an economist, Will?"

"It's a matter of interpretation, Robert. Are you going to be okay?"

"I'm fine, Will. I've been fine for a long time."

"Just in case I don't come back, Robert, if anything happens to your benefits because of undeclared income, just go see Mr. Kenny at the Royal Bank. He'll take care of everything."

Will put the transmission in drive and slowly pulled away. There wasn't much traffic. He drove through Parkdale and up Roncesvalles Street. He went up Black Creek Drive to Highway 400. Then north, to Highway 11. He kept driving north. He watched the day begin over the rock and snow and evergreens that spotted the side of the highway. The evergreens had freed themselves of snow and ice. The north was leaving winter behind. The sky was blue with ribbons of cloud dancing in the wind. He stopped once for gas and a coffee. He bought three bottles of water for the truck. He drove an hour past North Bay, then turned off the highway. It was wild country. Narrow, ungraded dirt roads. The old Ford bumped and creaked. Will slowed down to fifty. He had to watch very closely. The signs would be small. He found the first road on Cobb's list. It had no name, just a number on a small green sign. It was the same for the next road. He drove until he crossed over the stone bridge. He made his first left. He drove for another thirty minutes and found the wood garage Cobb mentioned, a rot-wood shack with a chain and padlock over two wooden doors. The road, in fact, ended with the garage. The truck was to go in the garage. That was the end of the plan. He didn't know when he would see Cobb again. He didn't have anyplace to go. There was no risk analysis, no projection into the future, no insight whatsoever into what came next. What came next was the product of a completely unstructured imagination.

He locked his clothes and computer in the truck and he locked the truck in the garage. He hid all the keys under a painted stone at the corner of the garage, where he had found the garage key. He picked up the bag with the books in it, and he walked into the bush holding on to Cobb's directions. This was an act of faith.

The signs weren't hard to see. The directions began with a footpath. Twenty minutes in, at a normal walking pace, he would see a small pile of stones, no higher than his knee. But he had to be careful, the directions warned. It might be buried under brush. He was to climb the hill behind the stones, on the other side would be a stream, which flowed to a lake. He was to follow the stream. It would lead him to their property.

After an hour, Will stopped to rest beside a large tree. As he sat there, he remembered what Polski had told him: A tree is a word in someone else's language. He closed his eyes and leaned against the trunk of the tree. His mind was left to play with the sounds around him, the wind in the trees branches, birds and small creatures. For the moments he rested under the tree, eyes closed, the stream inside him was the same as the stream outside of him. He got up and started walking again. In a short time, he came to a simple cabin. He walked around to the front, where there was a beautiful lake. There were no other buildings around the lake. No docks. He assumed he was in the right place, so entered the cabin. There was no heat, but there was a pot-bellied stove that was cold to the touch and a pile of wood in the corner.

The first thing Will did was build a fire. Then he retrieved one of the pots from under the sink, went to the lake, broke the ice and pulled up a pot of water. He returned to the cabin with the pot and placed it on the pot-bellied stove, then he went over to the cupboard and looked for tea. It was time to break his fast. There were a number of tin boxes in the cupboard, one had tea bags and one had sugar. There were mouse droppings all around. He took out the tins and a metal tea cup. He went outside and washed the cup with snow. When the water boiled he put the cup into the pot and filled it half full of water. He dropped in a tea bag and two pinches of sugar. He jiggled the cup. It tasted fine. He went back over to the cupboard to look for plates. There were none. There cans of stew and beans. There was a can opener. He opened a can of beans and placed it directly on the stove. The fire roared in the stove and anything placed on it would heat up quickly. In a few minutes, Will was eating beans with his fingers. They didn't taste bad. It was his first meal in a week.

He took off his jacket, his shoes, and his socks. His feet were wet from walking through the woods. He looked around. The cabin had big windows. There was one large table with eight chairs and four bunk beds at the back. It was a hunt camp. There was a note on the table, and the instructions it contained were clear. He would see the vision in the world when he was ready to see it. It would begin when he was not looking for it. He would see something from the vision, and then, shortly after that, something else. When he was certain that the vision had started, he was to leave the cabin and make the journey to his vision. *A vision is always a journey*, Cobb wrote in his note. *It has been this way since the beginning of time.*

Will sat and stared at the fire. The structure of time dissipated. They must have known this ten thousand years ago, he thought, the simple and elegant rhythms of firelight. There was never the exact same flicker, never the exact same plume of smoke. There was such a deep and peaceful presence in the fire, its crackling sound drowning out the noises from the forest. As the day turned to night, the air in the cabin took on a chill. When the night settled in and darkness surrounded the cabin, Will put on his socks, which had dried beside the stove, and he put on his shoes. He stepped out, into the night. He walked to the shore of the lake with the pot. He filled it with water. The night sky was brighter than he had ever seen. Stars filled it. He stood and stared at time's map until the cold forced his return to the cabin. He made one more cup of tea then lay down on one of the bunks at the back of the cabin.

He slept in short spells. The cold woke him up. The sounds from the forest woke him up. At one point in the night, he heard movement on top of the cabin. He didn't know what it was. It frightened him. He sat up in bed, heart beating quickly. He remembered what Cobb had told: That fearful things were in the world because there was fear in people. It comforted him and he fell back asleep.

He woke later in the night. The light woke him up. The moon was full and so bright it was like a spotlight shining into the cabin. He stared at it the same way he had stared at the firelight, in awe and wonder. While he was up, unsure what time it was, or when the morning would come, he put another log onto the embers in the stove, then he crawled back into bed. From bed he looked at the moonlight on the floor. The hatchings in the window made a shadow in the shape of a cross on the floor. The way the light stretched it made an uncanny resemblance to a crucifix. His back tingled. His was suddenly aware — the moon was the bright light, the shadow was the crucifix, and the note over on the table was from Cobb, who had spoken to the crow — a bright light, a crucifix, a crow. The vision had started. He sat up in bed and stared at the light on the floor. He resolved to set off at dawn. He slept no more that night.

He made tea and beans for breakfast. He ate. He laced up his shoes and opened the door. The sun was just coming up behind the cabin. He walked down to the lake and touched a large stone. He said to himself, "A stone, a crucifix, a bright light, and a crow." He crouched for a moment. The morning stillness was cracked by the wretched sound of a crow. Will looked up and saw the crow perched high above him on the branch of a winter-bare birch. It was a powerful omen. He felt alive in a simple and elemental way, completely alive, the way he had felt when he had awakened in his dormitory twelve months earlier. He followed the snow trail beside the stream all the way to the dirt road and then, like an idiot, he turned around again and walked back to the stream. He bent down and touched his fingers to the water, and said to himself, "A stream, a stone, a crucifix, a bright light, and a crow." He headed back to the dirt road. The morning passed way.

What would constitute a bear for the sake of the vision? His mind began to play tricks with him. If he made it back to a diner in a town and read in the newspaper about the spring bear hunt, would that be a part of his vision in the world? And what of the cross? The hatching in the window by moonlight was only the concept of a crucifix. He stopped dead in his tracks. He opened the book bag he had with him and shuffled through it quickly. He pulled out the crucifix he had stolen from Mrs. Duncan's rooming house. He stood holding it in his hand. His vision was coming into the world. Cobb had told him the truth. He remembered a priest's sermon about a person being the sum of his thoughts and feelings. His mind was electric. Everything was so clear, so perfectly clear. It was all starting to make sense. He walked on, into the afternoon, with a cool spring wind pushing through the woods and giving the trees the breath they needed to speak their words.

The dirt road cut through the rock terrain. He took breaks and sat at the side of the road. He hadn't seen another person since the coffee he had bought the day before. As he walked the long dirt road he came to some sense of what arduous and back-breaking work clearing the northern woods and levelling the terrain must have been. They must have worked from sun-up to sundown, ate their meals in the bush, and even slept in the bush, at least in the spring and fall, or maybe all year, he thought, in bush camps. Before the roads there were the rivers. The country had first been explored by canoe. Canoes were the first commercial vehicles — unlicensed, uninsured, but commercial nonetheless, built for the purpose of transporting people and goods. Where the rivers ended, they had portaged. They had picked up their canoes, tied their goods to their backs and trekked through the woods until they found the next river. There were no signs except what the sun, wind and water said to the trees, the stones and the earth. That was all they needed. Nothing had to be written down. The directions were all around them. They just had to be seen.

Will felt hungry and tired, but he was possessed of some spirit that forced one foot ahead of the other in a steady progression. Whatever the spirit was, it preferred the woods around it, the sky above and the earth beneath. He came across no clue of anyone in the wilderness with him — no vehicles, no voices, no distant smell of woodsmoke. He was alone.

He thought about his year in Parkdale. He remembered that he had stopped the flow of his life to follow his vision. The whole thing suddenly seemed hilarious to him, as though he were living in a dream. None of it made sense, but it didn't seem to matter anymore. He realized there was knowledge to be had just in the pursuit of a dream, as he knew that poverty was the inability to see your dreams in the world. He thought about the core belief of 1109897 Ontario Inc., that people would one day pay to breathe. He felt bad, but he remembered his dream journey had been beautiful. He'd seen so many wonderful things, so many wonderful people. It was almost better to live your life in a dream, he thought. Maybe that was the purpose of the vision, to make him human, weak, vulnerable. To show him the world from the bottom up, from tangled roots to twisted branches, from his naked imagination outward. He was just grateful for the whole thing, the seasons he had lived in Parkdale. He was worth a lot of money, and his wealth was growing daily, building out from itself, like a living organism. He was less than a year out of school and, he thought, how could any science that uses equations with human behaviour as a variable even be a science? It was all just a sham. Economics was a sham. It was like some unknown place out there in the bush, a place where only a single imagination was dreaming. There was no need for law. Conflict can't arise where there was only one dream.

The day began to slip away. The sun inched lower. Will didn't know how far he was from the main highway. He didn't know how much longer he would have to walk the dirt roads in the bush. He might be walking them all night, the roads illuminated by moonlight and starlight. He wasn't afraid. Fear could not take root in him anymore. He was prepared to sleep by the side of the road if he became too tired. Before he was put to that test, he saw a large black bear. At first he thought the bear wasn't real. He thought that he somehow dreamed the bear, he just kept walking toward it. The bear lumbered into the bush and disappeared. He walked up to where the bear had gone into the woods and saw broken sticks and a clear path into the brush. The bear was real.

Farther up the road, he thought, I walked toward a bear. I'm fearless. The vision has made me fearless. He heard a grunt behind him. He froze. He heard the grunt again. He turned around. The bear had come out of the woods a short way down the road. It stared at him. He stared at the bear. Four cubs emerged. They must have been tucked in the bush the whole time. He stood still, half expecting one of the cubs to have purple flowers in its mouth. The mother bear guided her cubs to the other side of the road. A truck drove up beside Will. He hadn't even heard it. It was a beat-up old Ford. He walked up to the passenger side and poked his head into the open window. It was an Indian girl about the same age as him.

"Aanii," the girl said.

"Aanii," he said back. It meant hello in the tongue of the Ojibwa people. Cobb had taught him the word.

"What are you doing out here?" she asked.

"I'm pulled by the magic of dream," he told her. "I'm on a journey."

"How long have you been on your journey?" she asked.

"I came to this road just after the sun this morning, but I have been on this journey for four seasons."

"What are you looking for?" she asked.

"Purple flowers," he said.

"What kind of purple flowers?" she asked. "What medicine are you making?"

"I don't know what kind of purple flower," he said.

"What was in your eye when you dreamed?" she asked. "Could you not see the flowers?"

"Any purple flower," he said.

She put the truck in park and got out. She walked around to him. She looked into his eyes. She was beautiful. She took him to the back of the truck and opened the cap. The bed of the truck was full of potted plants and flowers. She pointed to the back and said, "I have violets."

He saw the purple leaf and started to cry. He said, "A bright light, a crucifix, a crow, a stone, a stream, a black bear and purple flowers."

"Are you finished your journey now?" she asked.

"I am," he said.

"Where are you going now?"

"Toronto."

"I can take you there," she said. "I have to deliver these flowers."

They got into the truck. The sun was going down. It was dark by the time they got to the highway.

They drove in silence for a long time. They stopped for coffee and gas and, when they were back on the highway, Will started to speak. He told her about his life as it had unfolded over the past year, every detail, up to and including Paddy's suicide. Somewhere, between the dirt road where she picked him up and Toronto, they pulled over at a rest stop and made love. It was his first time, he told her as they lay beside the potted flowers in the bed of the truck, tucked between two sleeping bags. She held him tightly. He looked out the small window of the truck. He could see the stars in the night sky.

"It was a vision by my interpretation," he said. "Love is the most basic human exchange."

"It's good medicine," she said.

DEBT

COBB WOKE WITH A clear mind, fully refreshed. The Costa Rican Talamancas were already up and about. They were making breakfast over an open fire. They were were, like Cobb, an ancient people. They had similarities in complexion, hair colour and bone structure. Cobb felt a connection to them. Miguel Sanchez, *abrigado y notario*, had put Cobb in touch with them.

The Talamancas were the same as the Mohawks and Ojibwas he knew in Ontario and Quebec. They wore blue jeans, no feathers, and they lived on reserves the government of Costa Rica had established in the late 1970s. They worked at trades such as logging, if they worked at all.

Life was humming all around Cobb. The rain forest was a living thing. It was dense and there were dangers that could only be overcome with the guidance of the Talamanca guides. Sunlight came through to the forest floor in shafts. The foliage was extremely thick. It was the most complex ecosystem Cobb had ever seen. In the three nights he had slept in the rain forest with the Talamanca guides he had seen monkeys, sloths, snakes, frogs — many of which could not even be touched because of poisons on their skin — and the largest and most frightening insects he had ever seen.

He had hired the three Talamancas to walk the land he and Will owned. They followed the maps Sanchez had given Cobb. One of the Talamancas spoke English. The other two spoke only Spanish. The land had to be walked every four months or so. They had to watch for squatters. Cobb was building the relationships 1109897 Ontario Inc. needed to make sure the job would get done even if he or Will could not be in the country, because there was no telling when Cobb would have to leave. He didn't like the feeling of being pinned down, although there was the distinct possibility that he might stay in Costa Rica. It depended on the reliability of the information he had received from Philmore, through Will.

Cobb and the Talamancas had taken a hallucinogenic the night before that only the Talamancas knew how to prepare. It was not for any reason that they would mix up magic tea and drink it; a Canadian Indian with land interests in their country was occasion enough. They drank it in the rain forest. Cobb could remember bits and pieces of the night before, but he could make no sense of them in his mind. He should have had a vision of his animal guide. The puma was a favoured guide among the Talamancas, but Cobb had no such visitation. He concluded that he was a free man, because he knew that a vision was a debt. His debt to society was paid — through Crow, over the year he had lived on parole in Parkdale.

Squatters were a serious concern in Costa Rica, where they followed old rules. Whoever used the land owned the land. Cobb thought this was pretty much how it should be. So the land would have to be watched by the Talamancas if Cobb left and went to another country. They were the only ones who could watch the land properly.

Cobb took a bowl of food from one of the Talamanca guides and found a log to sit on. As he looked around, he was stunned by the beauty of everything around him. His eye caught a hummingbird coloured like a dozen ribbons tied together. At first he thought it was a large insect, but then he saw that it was a bird by the way it interacted with the flowers, and the way it hung in the air, its wings moving faster than what could be seen, extracting its sustenance from the heart of a purple flower the likes of which he had never seen. He thought, It's all so beautiful, this world.

After eating, they continued to hike the land, finishing late in the day. They jumped into a pickup truck, two of the Talamancas in the cab, and Cobb and one of the Talamancas in the open bed, the wind blowing their long black hair in all directions. They drove for a couple of hours. The Talamanca guides let Cobb off at the furnished home Sanchez had rented for Cobb, a small bungalow in Atenas. Cobb took a short nap when he got there. He slept a dreamless sleep until the telephone rang. It was Miguel Sanchez. "Please, Senior Cobb. Come to my office. There is some news."

Cobb got up and went to visit his *abrigado y notario*. He walked down steep sidestreets — Atenas was a mountain town. Most buildings on the city square were built into sloped land. It took him only ten minutes to make it to the city square, which was a small park bordered by streets and green benches.

The Mass was just over in the big church in the city square, and many people exited the church, coming down the stairs and into the city square. Costa Ricans were serious Roman Catholics. The Talamancas had told their history to Cobb. It was similar to his, except their imperial visitors were Spanish, not French — black robes nonetheless. The Spanish had preferred death by blade and gunpowder to death by smallpox — or perhaps they just weren't as good at genocide as their fellow Europeans — but the Talamancas had assured Cobb that many of their people had died, and that the Spanish were efficient with their weapons.

There was an Internet café on the other side of the city square, a small well-kept place that served the best coffee Cobb had ever tasted. The coffee beans were grown by the owner of the cafe. Cobb had gone in several times to send e-mails to Will, back in Toronto. 1109897 Ontario Inc.'s money was accessible through a small bank on yet another side of the city square.

Cobb went into the café and sat down at a computer. The woman who owned the café with her husband brought him a coffee. He typed a quick e-mail to Will: *Surveyed the land with the Indians and everything is okay. I'm going to stay here for a while. Cobb out.*

Cobb drank his coffee quickly and paid the proprietor. Cobb knew he was close. With Crow gone from his life, with what was born in his mind and passed in his mind gone, his heart, like any normal heart, set itself to love and the gentler things in the world. For him this meant Fatima.

Cobb crossed the city square. He went down a long street, down an alley, through a door, up a staircase, to a hallway, and then to a door marked: *Miguel Sanchez, Abrigado y Notario*. Cobb walked through the door and an attractive, copper-skinned young clerk came out to meet him. She spoke in Spanish and Cobb just nodded his head. She kept speaking until she knocked on an office door. There was a sound. She opened the door, delivering Cobb to Miguel Sanchez, who, at the age of seventy, had the quiet air of a benign magistrate, a gentle and humane disposition.

Sanchez promptly stood and shook hands vigorously with Cobb. He put a hand on Cobb's shoulder and offered tobacco and liquor. He liked to drink Mesqual, and the tobacco he smoked was hand-rolled from a farm for which he did some work. Cobb declined, though the gestures of kindness were not lost on Cobb, who had moved a lot of his business Miguel's way. It was a symbiotic relationship. Cobb was going to need friends in Atenas, and Sanchez was well known and respected. That's how business got done in Atenas.

Sanchez sat down only after Cobb had refused everything that was offered him, including an early supper that his assistant could prepare for them. He got right to business, handing Cobb cheque stubs from deposits to the bank along the city square, payments from the Costa Rican government on 1109897 Ontario Inc.'s land for conservation holdings. Cobb looked at all the figures and then handed the papers back to Sanchez. "Good," he said. "And the other thing?"

Sanchez folded his hands and smiled as widely as his face would let him. "We have news, Señor Cobb. Very good news. Our agents have picked up a trail in San Jose. It seems, Señor Cobb, that the woman is in Costa Rica."

Cobb stood to leave.

"What about the bananas?" Miguel asked.

"My man in Canada will look at the business plan," Cobb said. "I'm not at liberty to decide about the bananas alone."

And with that, Cobb departed the office of Miguel Sanchez, *abrigado y notario*. He said goodbye to the copper-coloured receptionist with black hair. He descended the stairs, pushed open the heavy door, and walked swiftly and purposefully out to the city square. In the park, he spotted a woman selling kittens out of a box. Cobb walked up to her, looked into her box, and grabbed a thin little black kitten by the pinch of skin on its neck. It hissed a little, so he held it up to his face and tapped it on the nose a couple of times until it became docile. He handed the woman some bills and walked across the park, out of the city square, across the street, and to the room he had rented. He would take care of the cat until he could give it to Fatima.

ACKNOWLEDGEMENTS

Thanks to my agent and friend, Sam Hiyate, for believing in me in the first place. Thank you to Bianca Spence for bringing this book to the front of the line at Cormorant, where they are committed to publishing new voices in Canada. Thank you to Emily Schultz for copyediting; Angel Guerra for his cover design and belief in this book; and Tannice Goddard for her beautiful work designing the text. My deepest thanks to my editor, Marc Côté, for taking a manuscript and making a book.

ANCIENT FOREST FRIENDLY

This book has been printed using
Ancient Forest Friendly, recycled stock.

The text within this book was typeset using Sabon,
designed by Jan Tschichold in 1967.
It was known as a Garamond variation.